William Hepworth Dixon

Royal Windsor

Volume IV

William Hepworth Dixon

Royal Windsor
Volume IV

ISBN/EAN: 9783337039073

Printed in Europe, USA, Canada, Australia, Japan

Cover: Foto ©Andreas Hilbeck / pixelio.de

More available books at **www.hansebooks.com**

ROYAL WINDSOR

BY

WILLIAM HEPWORTH DIXON

VOLUME IV.

Third Edition.

LONDON:
HURST AND BLACKETT, PUBLISHERS,
13 GREAT MARLBOROUGH STREET.
1880.

LONDON:
PRINTED BY STRANGEWAYS AND SONS,
Tower Street, Upper St. Martin's Lane.

CONTENTS

OF

THE FOURTH VOLUME.

ROYAL WINDSOR.

CHAPTER I.

HOUSE OF STUART.

1603.

THE Divine Catastrophe of the house of Stuart—to revive a famous phrase—covers the history of Windsor Castle, from the coming in of James the First, to the expulsion of his male descendants, in the persons of James the Second, and the wandering prince whose followers called him James the Third. It is the tale of an attempt to govern England for the benefit of a party and a sect.

Through all this drama, Windsor was the camp, the council-chamber, and the head-quarters of events. Here, the government of that party and sect was framed, and here the government of that party and sect was overthrown.

James Stuart, sixth in descent from that Scottish prince who had sung his love-lay in the Devil's tower, was third in descent from that Margaret Tudor who had been sent to Stirling in the hope of some day placing over one head the Scottish and English crowns. Thanks to Elizabeth's sacrifice, he came in like a son succeeding to his family estate; not a single shot being fired—hardly a single voice being raised—against his coming in. Some prudent men, like Raleigh, had dreamt of making terms with him; but the exuberant loyalty of his people had disdained to ask for either oath or bond. He came in free. Unhappily he was a man unfit for such a trust. Ignorant of England, he mistook the times in which he lived, thinking they were ebbing back when they were flowing on. In Bacon's words, he was a prince, not of the future, but of the past.

After ambling round his capital, he arrived at Windsor, where he settled in the royal house; to wait the coming of his wife, to hold a festival of St. George, to entertain ambassadors from foreign powers, and fix the principles on which he meant to reign.

Windsor delighted him, not because the air was sweet, the pile extensive, and the landscape wide, so much as because the towers were ancient, and the game was plentiful. In roaming through long galleries he could dream of the middle ages, and imagine himself a feudal king. The park was handy, and well stocked. Though idle, he could get up early to enjoy his sport. Not that he cantered, like Elizabeth, after stags; still less, like Henry, after wild boar. His pleasure was to shuffle after conies with a stick, or bring down partridges with a hawk; he had no nerve for going at the wilder game.

In spite of some good qualities, James was a poor pretender to the name of man. His ways were hard to bear, even by those who clung to him for bread. He never washed; in eating, he forgot his stomach; and in drinking, easily lost his legs. Coarse jests were current at his board, and in his closet; filth like that which Jonson was not ashamed to set before him on the Windsor stage. Ladies who saw him at table for the first time, turned from the sight in shame. Men smiled and shrugged their shoulders, saying they must make the best of a bad thing. In spite of his behaviour, he had reading enough to chop logic; wit enough to quirk and pun. Divinity was his weakness; but he liked to tackle policy, and peer into the secrets of medicine. When tired of chasing rabbits and tippling whisky, he sat down and wrote, under the idea that his pen was master of both prose and rhyme. Few critics praised his style, yet he was sometimes shrewd of phrase ; and though his verses grated and spluttered, they were not more rugged than the rhymes produced by other singers beyond the Tweed. A lenient judge pronounced him a learned fool. If bred in some lonely manse, and held to duty in his native dale, he might have left behind him the name of a canny and a clever man. His misery was that he was born to thrones, and that he came to Windsor in the days of Shakespere and Bacon to occupy Elizabeth's place.

Down to the hour of his arrival in Windsor, his life had been a daily lie. Born of a catholic mother, christened by a catholic priest, and swaddled by a catholic nurse, he had been driven by policy to conceal his creed, to sit under Calvinist preachers, and appear a docile pupil of the Kirk. Hypocrisy had sunk into his soul. When thinking of Windsor, he had fancied that, on reaching the sanctuary of St. George, he would be free to speak his mind, and even to impose his views on other folk, as had been done by Cardinal Pole. But Cecil warned him not to march too fast. England disliked extremes.

Opposed no less to the school of Parsons than to the school of Brown, a great majority of the English people only wanted to live in peace; to till their soil and weave their cloth, to press their apples and net their shores, unscared by any foreign prince; to woo and wed, bring up their youngsters, and hear the gospel preached, without the license of a foreign priest. That was the temper of four in five of his new subjects. But if roused by menaces of either prince or pope, they would be up in arms. The king, thus warned, held back in fear; but only for a little while. His own opinions would have startled people in the days of Edward the Third. He held that England was a feudal country, which he had a right to govern as a feudal king. This right in crown and sceptre he held to be ' divine.'

All men except himself saw clearly that the reign of feudal kings was over. Henry and Elizabeth had done their work, and closed their epochs. Freer times were coming in; the sword was yielding to the law. No theory could stay the coming in of light. The dawn had come, with liberty in her wake. No power on earth could force them back. Under a national prince, liberty might have entered on her kingdom by some other path than over battle-fields and scaffolds; but she would have come as certainly as light succeeds to darkness, and maturity succeeds to youth.

The seeds of change had long ago been sown; here, in the poet's prison; there, at the martyr's stake; sown by men like Surrey in the Norman tower, by men like Testwood under the Castle wall. A later crop was being sown, in fields less tragic to the eye, but not less fruitful to the mind; here, by a poet in the queen's gallery; there, by a student on the queen's terrace; here again, by a state-founder in the queen's ante-room. In plays, in tractates, in sea-adventures, this new crop of change was being sown; and every man in Windsor and out of Windsor saw this preparation for a future harvest, save the king.

In passing from the Tudor tower along the terrace to the Little park, James might have read the evidence of change. His castle was a type of feudal things, a pile of stones which every one was trying to preserve; yet Windsor Castle, like the lowlier structures in the hollow, was submitting to the laws of growth. Where was the Plantagenet fortress, with solid front of rock butting above a rugged scarp? That front was broken by the

Private stair, and brightened by the Tudor tower. That scarp, once steep enough to defy assault, was levelled for a lady's walk. Children were playing on the slope. Formerly a Norman stronghold, Windsor was becoming an English home.

From Berwick to Windsor, James might have seen these signs of growth; but he possessed no skill in reading histories in stone. Under his eyes, heroic rule lay dead, never to revive until the English race has perished from the earth. Free thought was won. Free thought was passing into free speech, and tending towards free act. Models of free states were being sought; here—in the past—in Greece, in Palestine, in Rome; there—in the mind of man—in Utopia, in Arcadia, in Bensalem. Some of the greatest intellects in England were projecting, and describing, these models of free states. On hearing of such researches, James exclaimed in wonder, ‘Hech! What are they about? Free states! Free states agree with monarchy as mickle as the de'il agrees wi' God.'

James marvelled all the more at these intellectual exercises, since he had himself put forth a tract, in which he had laid down his theories of public law as limited by kingly right. Princes, he had told the world, are like to gods, who never can be judged by men. A race apart, they have been chosen and anointed for their seats. By a divine commission, older than the oldest church, higher than the highest court, they have a right to lay their hands on what they want. All the fantastic theories of Filmer, Fern, and other sycophants, appeared on James's page. Denying history, he said the crown can never be forfeited by a reigning prince. In spite of Rufus, John, Bolingbroke, and Richmond, he declared that the line of English kings can never be changed. Statutes notwithstanding, he asserted that kings could tax and toll as pleased them; that the soil, and all that grows on it, were theirs: vineyard and pasture, farmstead and granary, young man and maiden. Kings, he stated, could do no wrong, and must not be accused of wrong. When they seemed harsh, their subjects must have patience. Even when they seemed criminal, their punishment must be left to Heaven. Kings, he maintained, were above the law. No earthly court had power to try, no earthly judge to sentence, an anointed prince. To James, this reasoning was complete: the earth is the Lord's; kings are the Lord's anointed; therefore the earth is theirs.

In no long time this syllogism, borrowed from his pages by the 'Saints,' was turned with a dramatic suddenness against his house.

Few readers had seen the king's tract, and those who glanced at his theories only laughed. That anybody in his senses would attempt to put them into practice, no one dreamt. But James, who was already sending secret emissaries to the Pope, made haste to show that he was ruling as a feudal prince. Of his own will, without consent of lords and commons, he revived, by proclamation, the Forest Laws—his first step on the road which led to the Divine Catastrophe of his house.

CHAPTER II.

THE LITTLE PARK.

1603.

JAMES introduced his feudal law at Windsor by enclosing the Little Park.

Two causes raised in him the wish to close this park. First, the townsmen—who, like Ford and Page, walked over his grass with dog and gun, and cleared off some of that smaller game which he most of all loved to hunt ; second, the strangers —who, like Nym and Pistol, hung about the stands, and laughed at his sport of racing after rabbits with a trail of gentlemen at his heels. By locking his park-gates he expected to preserve his conies, and to silence his critics in the tavern yards. Shut out that mob of burgesses and tramps, and who, save his own keepers, would be able to see his sport ? Who, save his own butlers, would have a chance of counting the contents of his bag ?

East of the Castle, on a ridge of chalk, ran the Little Park—a high and lonely stretch of grass and trees, looking into the deer-course and across the river, but unseen from any other site except the Castle leads. It was a park, and something more: the favourite hunting-ground of Queen Elizabeth, and the scenery of her 'Merry Wives.' Here stood Herne's oak; here dropped the Fairy dell. Here ran the elm-walk planted under Elizabeth's eye. Tree and sward were steeped in a romantic light. Hundreds of visitors came to see the oak and dell by which the elves had danced, while Falstaff roared with pain, and Fenton slipped away with 'sweet Anne Page.' The Little Park was a poetic place. But James cared nothing for the Merry Wives. Shut out these Fords and Pages, Nyms and Pistols, from that ridge, and he might take his sport in peace—supposing always that such burgesses as Ford and Page, such 'loose companions' as Nym and Pistol, were content to be shut out.

Would they retire and make no sign?

These forest laws which James invoked at Windsor were obsolete. For more than sixty years, no man had been hung for breaking through a fence, or bringing down small game. The code was dead: leaving in the minds of men the memory of a brutal system which had come to be a theme for prank and jest. Turn once more to the 'Merry Wives,' that perfect picture of Windsor thought and feeling at the moment when the Stuart dynasty came in.

'*Shallow.*—You have beaten my men, killed my deer, broke open my lodge.

'*Falstaff.*—But not kissed your keeper's daughter.

'*Shallow.*—Tut! a pin! This shall be answered.

'*Falstaff.*—I will answer it straight—I have done all this. That is now answered.

'*Shallow.*—The council shall know.

'*Falstaff.*—You will be laughed at.'

Even so; the atrocious forest laws had come to that. Offences which had once been punished by death, were matters for tavern jests. Shallow begins and ends with words. Instead of going to the council to 'be laughed at,' he leaves his injuries to umpires: to his parson, to his neighbour Page, and to his host of the Garter. That scene was but a mirror of all rural life. People had forgotten that in other days, to shoot a stag had been regarded as a worse offence than to slay a man.

These laws were now to be revived, not in Berkshire only, but in every county of the land, where James possessed a park, or had the usage of a park. Nobody was to leap a fence, to snare a rabbit, or to hawk a bird. At first, the yeomen only laughed. Riding across country to cheer the king, halting at roadside inns to drink his health, they heard of this new proclamation, and received it as a joke. Not leap a fence, not catch a bird! When they were warned to wait and see, they roared in merriment, and drained more beakers to the royal wag.

A fence ran round the Little Park, two miles in circuit; but the pales were only stakes and boards, which every yokel in the town could over-leap. Three gates led into the preserves: one gate from the queen's terrace, a second from the deer-course, a third from the market-place. The first path was a private entrance, but the other paths were free. Shakespere, coming up from Datchet Mead, entered by the deer-course. Through the town gate, Falstaff had stolen to Herne's oak, followed by the Merry Wives. The walks and swards were as free to men and maids as they were free to ouphes and elves. No one had ever heard of a time when they were closed. All strangers were allowed to roam about. But for that freedom, no man would have heard of the Hunter's tree, nor learnt the legend of the Fairy dell. Windsor would have lost one of her greatest charms. Though Queen Elizabeth had hunted in the park, she had never dreamt of shutting her neighbours out. Every lad in Windsor had seen her majesty, bow in hand, standing behind a tree, and bringing down her buck. Under her reign all paths had been open to the holiday-maker with dog and gun.

This right of way was not the only right to be disturbed by shutting up the Little Park. Time out of mind poor people had enjoyed the right of fuelling in the park and forest. No statute gave that right, just as no statute gave the right of gleaning in a cornfield; usage older than the longest memory, forming part of an unwritten code, was taken by the churl and housewife as a right. No one denied the king his cuttings, but when his yards were stacked, poor people claimed their chips and barks. After the reaper comes the gleaner; after the woodman comes the churl.

By shutting up his park the king might save his rabbits and sell his lops and tops. But could the park be safely closed? James shrank from the risk of meeting men with dogs and guns; he shrank still more from the risk of meeting mobs of laundresses and ale-wives. He had a mortal dread of seeing an urchin cross his path. A crowd of women searching for their winter fuel would be sure to have some urchins in their wake. They might refuse to run away; they might accost him in the park; they might startle him into fits. Before he ventured to close his park gates, he ordered two experiments to be tried elsewhere, at a perfectly safe distance from the Tudor tower.

Enfield Chase and Brigstoke Park were chosen for these trials. Chase and park were closed under his new rules, and men were sent in to cut down wood, and carry away the tops and lops. If no no one stirred, the king's aggression might be called his right. Some stir was made. At Enfield Chase a mob of women gathered round the carters. Why, these women asked, were they carrying off the poor man's fuel? For the king's use, replied his men. 'Tish!' returned the women, 'the king is not at Enfield lodge.' While living there, they thought he had his claim to fuel from the chase; but if he chose to lodge elsewhere he had no right to make his penny of their winter fires. Were they to die of cold? Who ever heard before of barks and twigs being sold by kings? In former days, when there was too much wood, a portion had been sold; but then the money had been distributed among the poor. That was the custom under Good Queen Bess. These hussies spake the truth, and claimed no more than they had always taken for their own. Gleaning and fuelling were relics of a time when hedger and ditcher had a property in the soil. But James, safe in the King's house at Windsor, allowed his case to be urged at Enfield with pike and gun. His troops cleared out the 'rioters.' Many of the jades were sent to prison; and the churls their husbands sat at their fireless hearths, cursing the strange king and his outlandish rules.

At Brigstoke the trial was more serious than at Enfield Chase. This park had been stocked with deer for the king's amusement; but his majesty said he must have the smaller game preserved. Sheriff and magistrate were ordered to see that his game was neither snared nor killed. His wood was also to be gathered up and sold. This challenge brought in graziers from the hillside and butchers from the town. Shut up the park and sell the lops and tops! What laws were these? No one in Elizabeth's days had done such things, and no one should begin to do them now. The graziers smashed the fences, while the butchers overturned the carts. 'Down with gates, down

with fences !' cried·the mob.   An ominous name
was heard—that name of 'leveller,'—which events
were afterwards to make so terrible to the king
and to his son.   But troops were moved into the
park, who swept these rioters from the ground :
the graziers to their cattle-runs, the butchers to
their market-stalls.   The county jails were filled,
and Brigstoke as a market-town was ruined.   Up
to that time Brigstoke had been a busy place,
with a good cattle-fair.   After the tussle in the
park, graziers ceased to bring their beasts into the
town, and the butchers moved into other shires.

The king was pleased with his success.   After
these trials, he might close the park under his
Castle wall ; close it, as he wished, 'to all men
under rank of peer, except some gentlemen of the
highest quality ; who would receive his license to
that end.'

His course was quickened by a slight domestic
scene.

When Anne, his consort, came to Windsor, he
insisted on her going out at once to see him hunt ;
and the good-humoured lady, though fatigued with
riding in the sun, walked with him into the Little
Park.   He placed her at the stand, where she
could overlook his sport.

Anne was a woman of the North, a daughter of the Dane. That coursing after rabbits with a pack of beagles struck her as a game for boys, not men ; and after looking on the scene some time in scorn, she snatched a cross-bow, singled out a buck, and brought his antlers to the ground. All faces turned on her. She had but just arrived, and every one was measuring her with his eye. Her aim was true, her bearing proud ; men smiled, and said she was a queen. But James felt sorely hurt. His wife, he thought, was shaming him, not before his courtiers only, but before the common herd—rascals who might mock him in their cups, and toast his consort as the better man.

Turning aside, he stood apart and sulked. His day was dashed. Anne, used to his ill-temper, turned on her heel, and going to her rooms in the Castle, left him to follow when his passion cooled. On his return, he called his secretary and signed his edict, closing the gates of his Little Park.

CHAPTER III.

THE QUEEN'S COURT.

1603.

LIKE all the Danish princes and princesses, Anne was a Lutheran, and her court at Windsor was expected to present the features and preserve the manners of an Evangelical court.

Fine eyes, fair face, and lissom figure — with a gleam of humour in her smile, a flick of lightning in her talk—made Anne a charming woman in the sight of every one at Windsor, except the king. James treated her with outward courtesy, but he feared her, even when professing to love her most. She had a tongue, and when he vexed her, she was free of speech. He vexed her very much—in great things and in small; the custody of her son, the doings of her servants, and the chatter of her fool. Of late they had seldom met, except to sneer and chafe. Anne was of higher mettle than her spouse ; and when he boasted of his crown, she answered stiffly that she was the daughter of a king. Though they were man and wife, father and mother of a royal race, they had begun to fall into separate ways of life. James kissed her cheek in public, but the ceremony done, they wandered back into their private rooms ; Anne to amuse her time with book and picture, dance and play ; James to tipple whisky, listen to coarse jokes, and rail against the weaker sex—the sex of Queen Elizabeth and Queen Anne. No 'secret room,' no 'private passage,' were required in the domestic intercourse of Anne and James.

Only two ladies came with Anne to Windsor. James brought in as many of his people as he pleased ; but he had told his consort, when he quitted her at Holyrood, that English ladies were so jealous of their rights, that if she had strange women near her person, they would never come to court. He had two objects in his mind; one personal, one political. Although a Scot, he undervalued Scottish beauty, and he wished his lairds to marry English wives. Those lairds were poor ; by marrying English girls they might grow rich. No southern lord, he thought, would dream of courting a Scottish bride ; therefore he wished his wife to leave her female fry at home. Of greater moment was his second purpose, which he carefully concealed. He wanted to surround his wife with women of his choice; women who would lead her gently on the road he wanted her to take. With deep regret she left her friends behind.

At Windsor she found the court which had been prepared for her by James; a court that struck her with amazement; equally on the male and on the female side.

England was rich in eminent men. Raleigh was nigh; Bacon was waiting for an audience; Grey was standing in the crowd; but these great men were left to saunter on the terrace, or linger in the ante-room, while sots like Lennox, or fools like Hay, were closeted with his majesty. Anne, though often frivolous, had a sense of nobler things. Among those who filled her ante-room, few of the men were with their wives; hardly any of the women were with their husbands. Cecil was here, but not his wife; Lady Rich was here, but not her husband; Cumberland was here, but not his wife; Lady Kildare was here, but Cobham, her husband, was in Kent; Southampton was here, but not Southampton's wife; Lady

Hatton was here, but not her husband, Coke. Suffolk and his partner lived under one roof, but scandal said that roof was as common 'as the North Road.' Anne raised her voice against such people being placed about her, and was not much pacified by being told that these lords and ladies were the greatest in the land.

To her the women were more offensive than the men.

First in the group stood Catharine, Lady Suffolk, partner of the fighting earl; a widow of Lord Rich before she married Suffolk. Catharine was past the prime of middle age, but she had managed to preserve her beauty and improve her wit: her rivals said, by means of charms and spells. She certainly toyed with magic, and kept her sorcerers much as she kept her domestic priests. She fawned on Cecil, she intrigued with Southampton. Sordid and unscrupulous, she sold her services to any one who could pay her price. No money ever passed her hand. With equal greed she swept into her heaps the smallest and the largest bribes; taking a ring from a page with as much glee as a casket from a prince; begging a place worth ten pounds a-year in the kitchen as keenly as a pension of five thousand marks a-year.

The gains of this bad woman laid the foundations of Suffolk House and Audley End.

Next to Lady Suffolk stood her daughter, Frances, the betrothed of Robert Devereux, nephew of Lady Rich. Though but a girl, Frances had been trained in all the villanies of her mother's school. What Lady Suffolk knew of evil, Frances, her daughter, also knew—the market-price of rank, of beauty, of compliance. Young in years, she was experienced in deceit. Not by any twist or wrench, but on the lines laid down in her mother's house, she grew into that monster of iniquity known to every one as the adulteress Lady Essex, and the poisoner Lady Somerset.

Hardly behind these reprobates came Penelope, Lady Rich. Penelope was a sister of Essex, a connexion of Elizabeth; yet her birth had not preserved her from the scandals of a reckless life. In earlier days, she had been the heroine of Sydney's verse. Greed of money had led her to marry Rich, nicknamed 'Rich Lord Rich;' and by that match she had become a close connexion of Lady Suffolk. Rich had proved a fool; his wife a jade. Soon after Sydney's death, she had flung herself into the arms of Blount, now become Lord Montjoy. Three of her children were disowned by her husband. The profligate lady, laughing in his face, admitted that their father was the handsome Irish deputy. To one of them she had impudently given the name of Montjoy.

No less singular were two other dames—Alice, dowager countess of Derby, and her daughter Anne, Lady Chandos. Alice, the dowager countess, was believed to have poisoned her husband. Though a matron past her prime, she had no objection to vend her smiles and sell such influence as she possessed at court. Lady Anne, her daughter, was no better than herself; in personal profligacy she was rather worse. It is not too much to say, that of all weak women in English story, Anne Stanley was the most unfortunate; it is hardly too much to say, that of all bad women in English story, Anne Stanley was the most abominable. One of her partners in wickedness, standing on the gallows with the rope about his neck, denounced her as 'the wickedest woman in the world.'

Some ladies of a better class, like Lady Bedford and Lady Pembroke, came to see the queen. These women were not only pure in life, but shared the queen's opinions as to politics and creeds. With them she could get on. Lady Bedford stayed with her. Lady Pembroke was too old; she came to Windsor for a day, and vanished with the day. The women who were meant to be about her, and to form her court, were mainly of the school of Lady Suffolk and Lady Rich.

Inquiry showed the queen that all these women of impure life were either open Papists, or suspected of being Papists in disguise. Were they at Windsor by design?

James had long been tampering with his consort's creed. At Holyrood he had urged her to give up her Lutheran service for the Kirk; that is to say, of outward and seeming service in the Kirk. At Windsor he began urging her to give up Calvinism for the English church. What next? Was she, an evangelical Danish princess, being driven by him along the way towards Rome? The festival of St. George might yield a clue.

Postponed from spring to summer, on account of her late arrival, the inaugural festival of the reign was to be held in pomp and state. Henry, her son, now heir-apparent, was to be knighted, in company with two reigning princes—Christiern of Denmark, and Friedrich of Würtemberg. As in the times of Bolingbroke and Richmond, this inaugural festival of the new dynasty was to express the genius of the coming reign.

Prince Henry was a boy of such rare promise, as to win more praise from judges of all kinds of excellence than any other Stuart, either before his birth or since his death. In figure he was tall and lithe ; the blood of Queen Elizabeth seemed to flush his face, the strength of Queen Elizabeth to nerve his arm. Eyeing the father and the son, men asked how such a shoot had sprung from such a tree? Keen rider, skilful pikeman, Henry, at the age of ten, was ready to begin his exercise in the field. Horses and arms were his delight; yet from his mother he had learned to love books and pictures, to practise music, to collect prints and medals. He had not been long in England ere he had made acquaintance with the poets. He cheered Ben Jonson, pensioned Drayton, patronised Sylvester. Donne and Chapman sang his virtues. Shakespere sketched him in Guiderius, the typical British prince. All lovers of their country looked to him as captain. Nottingham loved the boy. Raleigh counted him a new Harry of Agincourt. Bacon set him down as the Cæsar of his Empire of Man.

Christiern, the queen's brother, was a bluff,

hard - hitting Dane, given to strong liquors and fierce onsets. In creed he was a Lutheran, with little reading, but no end of heat and dash. Since Vasa's death, the Danes had come to the front as champions of the Evangelical cause; which Christiern understood, not in this or that dogmatic sense, but on the broad political ground of independence. To James, his brother-in-law, he had been used to give a bantering sort of patronage. Danes and Scots had seldom been good neighbours, and the hope of war between them was extremely popular with the Danes. Queen Anne had brought the Orkneys and the Shetlands as her dowry to the Scottish crown; and many of the Danes were eager to regain those groups, which they regarded as the outworks and defences of their naval power. The kings had little to unite them, save their common kinship to Queen Anne. To Christiern, James's policies and pastimes seemed ridiculous. Kingcraft! What had a king to do with craft? His business was to fight, and tell the truth, not to chatter and equivocate like a priest. When he went out for sport, the Danish king's pleasure was to mount his horse and shoot his stag, not scamper after hares, and · bring down partridges with a hawk. He loved the reek of powder, and the flash of sabres stirred his blood. At sport, in which no man was allowed to fire a gun, he laughed with the uproarious mockery of an old Norse god.

After James arrived at Windsor, Christiern paid more attention to his brother-in-law. A king at Holyrood was not to be compared against a king at Windsor. In the north, James had always been a borrower, yet he had not been able to equip a fleet. Nobody thought of him, unless in reference to some border raid. At Windsor, he disposed of regiments and squadrons. He might save Ostend. A word from him, and Grey might press into the Rhine duchies—Raleigh might fling his vessels on the Spanish ports. One resolute decision on the part of James might turn the scale. A man so placed was master of the war.

Friedrich of Würtemberg, the second reigning prince selected for a stall, was Shakespere's 'German duke.' He was to be invested on the strength of Elizabeth's promise, given to him more than ten years ago.

Henry, Christiern, Friedrich! These were excellent names; pleasant to the queen and to the people; yet they were hardly to be received as tests of preference. None of these princes could be said to have been really chosen by the king. Who were his other knights—the men of his own choice, the mirrors of his mind, the pledges of his reign?

CHAPTER IV.

THE KING'S KNIGHTS.

1603.

Two of the king's knights were English, two were
Scottish.   Pembroke and Southampton were his
English choice, Lennox and Mar his Scottish choice

William Herbert, third earl of Pembroke, and
Henry Wriottesley, third earl of Southampton,
seemed to be chosen by the king on the principle
of facing two ways—of running with the fox, and
crying with the hounds.   Pembroke, who was
neither a Calvinist nor a Catholic, had so little of
the bigot in his nature, that fanatics called him a gay
young spark, without a sense of the religious life.
Southampton, like his father, and his father's father,
was a Romanist; and, in spite of his lax morals, an
obedient servant of his church.   Neither Pembroke
nor Southampton had much independent claim to
notice; yet the names of both were widely known

to fame. One was—the other had been—Shake-spere's friend.

Pembroke was barely twenty - three. Like Philip, his younger brother (soon to become a favourite, and to win the Garter), he was fond of plays ; and from the time of his first appearance in Elizabeth's court, he had sought the company of wits and poets. Wit and poetry were indeed the heritage of his race. Mary, his mother, was a mistress of the pen as well as being ' the subject of all verse.' Sydney, his uncle, had left one of the greatest names in poetry since Surrey's time : his ' Astrophel and Stella ' being almost as popular as ' Fair Geraldine.' Pembroke's own verses, whether amative or pastoral, had their day of favour ; and many of his songs were set to music by such masters in the craft as Linacres and Lawes. George Herbert was a member of his family ; Herbert of Cherbury was also of his blood. His house at Wilton was a temple of the liberal arts. Taken by itself, Wilton was a charming spot ; but grounds and galleries had alike been touched with the magician's wand. His garden was Arcadia. In his galleries stood a theatre, on the stage of which the best productions of his time were played. Sydney had paced those grounds; Shakespere had trod that stage.

Early in life Pembroke had won the heart of Spenser. He was kind to Jonson; Massinger was a dependant of his house. Yet his abiding interest to mankind springs from his fellowship with Shakespere, and his admiration for the poet's verse. That fellowship, that admiration, led to his name being printed on the foreground of Shakespere's works; a chronicle to outlive monuments of bronze and pyramids of stone.

Rich, noble, handsome, generous, Pembroke had the love of many persons, the respect of nearly all. He had the singular merit in a courtier of wanting nothing from the crown. Spending like a prince, he made no merit of his outlay, even though his charge was frequently for the public good. Such men were new to James; yet Pembroke never rose into the rank of favourite. He had no single taste in common with the king. Pembroke was gay where James was dull; Pembroke was lavish where James was mean; Pembroke sought the society of women where James preferred the company of dogs. In policy and in creed they stood on opposite sides. Pembroke was attached to the English church, which he regarded as the mainstay of English independence. He detested Spain, and all the works of Spain. Like the great poet, he was passionately patriotic, and his leanings were in favour of the policy of Raleigh, Grey, and Vere.

Different as night from day was his colleague, Southampton; a companion fated to sit beside him in St. George's choir, and live with him on Shakespere's page.

More than ten years had passed since Shakespere, struggling into public notice, had inscribed to the catholic peer a tale in rhyme, called ' Venus and Adonis.' It was usual for a poet to select a patron of his own opinions. Spenser had chosen Grey, a protestant of protestants. Shakespere in that early time had chosen Southampton, a catholic of catholics. One year after his production of ' Venus and Adonis,' he had printed ' Lucrece,' which he had also dedicated to Southampton; but with such a difference in the wording as implied that in the meantime he had been taken into service. ' What I have done is yours; what I have to do is yours; being part of all I have devoted yours.' About that time the dramatist wrote his comedy of ' Sir John Falstaff and the Merry Wives.' Can any man doubt that his abuse of the Lutheran prince at Windsor was a part of what he had 'devoted' to the catholic earl? Spenser had written of Grey as the pillar of his life, through whose 'large bounty' he was able to live. Though prone to magnify his office, Shakespere never guessed how much he had to give in exchange for smiles or pence. 'Lucrece' ran through edition after edition, carrying his patron's name into every county of the land. Then, year by year, had flowed from his pen a stream of sonnets, dealing with topics and emotions of the day—of singular value for the poet's life. This verse was buoyed by many hopes and burdened by many fears. One day the poet urged his patron to take a wife. Next day he chid him for his evil courses, and anon accused him of the grossest breach of faith. Yet all the while he strove, by artifice of words, to find excuses for his patron's faults.

> 'Those petty wrongs that liberty commits,
> Thy beauty and thy years full well befits.'

That some of Shakespere's excuses for his patron were sarcastic, every reader feels. When he compared him to a pretty woman, whose follies and offences might be overlooked in tribute to a dainty face—

> 'And for a woman wert thou first created'—

everyone sees that he is not comparing him to a woman like his own Imogen, his own Isabella, but to some wanton and fantastic creature of the stamp of Lady Rich.

These sermons in sonnets had continued till the time which wrecked so many friendships—that of the days succeeding to the Island voyage. At that turning-point of so many lives, the sonnets stopped, never to be resumed; and not without some bitter thoughts and some accusing words. But they had done their office, and Southampton, though suspected and unpopular, was a noted man.

Such were the English knights of James's choice. In naming Pembroke, James imagined he was buying off the Puritans; in naming Southampton, he imagined he was securing the Jesuits. That was his 'craft.' These sectaries were his dangerous classes :— of the English nation, who were neither Puritans nor Jesuits, he took no heed.

Lennox, the first of his Scottish knights, was not simply a Papist, but the agent, in James's court, of Cæsar and the Pope. Anne knew him but too well : a man of blood, a man of bad faith, a man of turbulent passions, who had thoroughly cowed the king. James feared his subject as a sparrow fears a snake. Lennox not only braved him to his face, but drove his servants from their posts. Once, in the king's sight, he had drawn his sword and pinned an officer to the wall. In pure contempt, he had carried off a royal ward by force, and married her, not only against the king's will, but against the ordinances of the Kirk. Strong in the support of Rome, of Spain, of Austria, he had carried everything in the Scottish court according to his will.

One Scot, and only one, was more offensive to the queen than Lennox. That man was Mar, the second of the king's Scottish knights. Mar was a darker, more imposing figure than the duke : a man of stronger passions—not so hasty with his tongue and sword—but of a steadier nerve and deadlier purpose. Mar had been at school with James ; but he had always kept his royal play-mate down. Sitting in kirk, and professing to be a Calvinist, he had chosen a catholic wife. Living in friendship with the king, he had entered into the Gowrie plot. By treachery and violence, he had got possession of James's son—a source of constant strife between the king and queen. ' Mar and his Papist wife are not fit guardians for our son,' stormed Anne. ' If you think so,' shuffled her husband, ' keep your fancies to yourself.'   But Anne was not a woman to hold her tongue, even when she was compelled to stay her hand.   On James riding from Holyrood, Anne had started for Stirling castle, where she had halted her company, and demanded the surrender of her son.   The ' Papist wife ' had refused to yield.   Anne fought against her with a woman's weapons — tears, fainting fits, and a mishap; and in the end she had gained her point.   Thus Henry was at Windsor by her side: first of that group of Stuart knights on whom so many eyes were fixed.

The queen was no more satisfied with the choice of Lennox and Mar than with that of Southampton.   Few people in her drawing-room knew much about the Scottish peers; but every one in Windsor knew Southampton as a rebel who had narrowly escaped the block.

Seated in her great chamber, Anne was giving audience and allowing the new-comers to kiss hands.   The women quizzed her sunburnt cheek, and marvelled at her riding in the heat of day without a veil.   But every one admitted that her eye was quick, her presence striking.   Most of the ladies in her circle were connexions of Essex, for whose name and cause she had a deep dislike.

The king had told her that the cause of Essex was their own ; but she had always fought against that view. How, she asked, could traitors to their queen be trusted ? Essex owed everything to the queen's bounty ; yet he had had the baseness to rise against her. Why expect him to be truer to a stranger than to his natural queen? Anne judged the [rebels with a woman's sense. On meeting Lady Rich, she marvelled how that profligate could have been the star of any honourable cause.

Southampton offered to explain his actions. She had not seen the man before ; but every one around her knew him as the hero of three or four humiliating anecdotes. Apart from Shakespere, everything about him had been more or less odious and contemptible. Every page at court had heard of his having been bundled out of the late queen's anteroom by an usher ; of his having raved about his birth and dignity; of his having paraded his scratched face and rumpled love-locks ; of his having sworn never to rest satisfied till the offending officer was dismissed ; of his having gone to the queen, who, on hearing both sides, had publicly thanked her servant for having taught the unmannerly peer to behave more decently in a lady's anteroom. Every lad in town had heard of Southampton being beaten in the street ; of his sneaking out of quarrels which his insolence had provoked ; and of his being hissed and flouted for his cowardice. In ten years, he had fallen so low that Shakespere, when he drew the character of Cloten, may have had the popular estimate of Southampton in his mind.

Standing near the queen's chair, Southampton offered to explain to her the mystery of the Essex rising, and to let her majesty understand how many great lords had taken part in that enterprise.

Anne stopped him with the words :

'I marvel much, my lord, that if so many great lords as you say, were in the action, that they did so little for themselves.'

'Madam,' he replied, 'the reason why we failed in that affair was this : our enemies turned the queen against us, so that we were forced to yield. If they had not turned the queen against us, not one of the contrary party, our private enemies, who were alone concerned, durst have shown his face.'

Grey, standing near the queen and catching these words, stepped forward, and assured her majesty that in any case, 'those of the contrary party' durst have done more than any of the rebels in that cause.

'You lie!' roared Southampton, in her majesty's presence, and in the hearing of all her court.

'How now, my lord?' said Anne, rising to her feet, her blue eyes flashing fire.

Fixing Southampton with her glance, she beckoned to the guard, and bade her officer arrest the disputants, remove them from her chamber, lodge them in separate towers, and station sentries at their doors.

CHAPTER V.

SPURIOUS PEACE.

1603–4.

THE peers being removed, Anne sent her usher to the king, with a report of what had passed, and a demand that he should hold a court of inquiry, and award such punishment to the offenders as would check all tendency to imitate their offence.

Anne felt with Grey, whose action in the rising she admired; but she had put him under guard in order to prevent a challenge, and a probable loss of life.

Though they were both of them young in years, Grey and Southampton were old in enmity. That enmity stretched back into their teens. Grey, a Protestant, if not a Puritan, had always stood across Southampton's path. A splendid rider and a deadly swordsman, he was endowed and trained for an ideal Master of the Horse. Elizabeth had chosen him from among a hundred candidates. Coveting that showy post, Southampton had sneered at Grey, and set on others to traduce him with the queen. Resenting these affronts, Grey had beaten his rival in the public streets. Their lives had been a duel. In Dublin, Grey had been subjected by Southampton to the shame of an arrest. Passing over to the Low Countries, he had sent a cartel to his rival, which that rival had refused to meet; alleging that the time was unsuitable, that his forces were in peril, and he could not leave them; that a pledge had been taken from him not to risk his life except in the queen's service. Grey had waited for him, knowing that he would have to fly from Dublin to the States. On his arrival, he had renewed his challenge in the bitterest scorn: 'Your coming hither shows your repentance of your cool answers. Neither disadvantage of time, peril, or promise, can now be pretended, and I call on you to right me.'

Southampton had no stomach for such righting. 'I refuse your challenge,' he had replied to Grey. In the opinion of his peers, Southampton was not entitled to refuse. Grey was of older family than himself. Seven or eight peerages vested in the Greys, some of them ducal, some of them dating from the time of Lion Heart. Southampton was an upstart, only one peer standing between himself and the pettifogger who had hunted Surrey to the block. To save his credit, he had written to Grey: 'Lest you think I dare not walk abroad for fear of you, I will ride an English mile out of the porte, with only unarmed attendants, wearing a sword and dagger which I will send to you. I will wait two hours, and defend myself against whoever offers.' Grey could only laugh. Wanting to fight his enemy like a soldier, point to point, he had no intention of provoking two mobs, like kernes at an Irish fair, into a free fight. Copies of these letters had been sent to London, where 'poor Southampton' had passed into a court by-word and a tavern jest.

On their return from the Netherlands, Southampton had put on airs of scorn, and ventured on saucy words. Grey, meeting him in the Strand, had beaten him a second time; for which disturbance of the peace he had been committed to the Fleet. In a few days he had been out, and at his post again. On finding that the rebels were about to rise, the queen had once more made him Master of the Horse, in which capacity he had played a leading part in crushing their attempt.

Anne felt that if the peers were left alone to settle the affair, blood was certain to be shed. James was no less angry with his wife than with his knight. The queen seemed taking up his rod. No doubt she had been grossly hurt, and he was bound to see her righted ; no less bound to do so for his own sake than for hers. Men who would give the lie in her presence, might dare to give the lie in his. Yet he disliked to have such work on hand. He wanted peace, and most of all in his own house. One of his delusions was to pose as a man of peace. A drum shook his nerves, a gun turned his stomach ; therefore, he pretended to the character of a pacific prince. What he supposed to be his virtue, was in fact his malady. Such peace as England loved — the peace of strength, of truth, of independence—stood beyond his range of thought. By peace he meant no more than silence and repose ; silence on every side, repose at any price. These articles he found were dear. Not only thanes and lairds, but grooms and barbers, had been used to play on his defect— braving and bullying, and pretending to touch their dirks under his royal nose. 'Nay, laddies, mak' it up ; nay, kiss and mak' it up,' he had whined. Knowing their master, they had pretended to huff and haw, and talk of having each other's blood. James had wept. 'Nay, mak' it up; I'll tak' the matter on myself.'

Taking such matters on himself was an expensive luxury. The price of peace ran high. On coming to Windsor he had greater need than ever to buy his laddies off. Most of the apartments near the Tudor tower were occupied by peers and gentlemen who had held them for many years, under warrants from the crown. Counting on his weakness, the laddies burst into these rooms, hustled the English tenants, and swore that his majesty would not be safe till such apartments were occupied by faithful Scots. Wild scenes took place, and some of his laddies narrowly escaped being hurled over the Castle wall. 'Peace, peace!' sighed James, going in between his old friends and his new; 'I'll tak' it on myself.' The storm got hushed, but ere the week was out, James had to pay the cost of that palace-peace.

What was a pacific prince to do with his wife's imprisoned lords? The outrage had been open, and a hundred persons had heard Southampton's words. Grey was not the man to miss so clear a chance. His enemy had escaped too often; now, he could punish him with the sanction of all honest men. James knew enough of the two prisoners to foresee the end if they were left to fight it out. Nor could he pass so gross an outrage on his wife. The queen was in a rage, unlikely to forgive the criminal, and James was bound to think of his own security no less than of her dignity and repose. He gave his orders for a council to be called next day.

The council met, and the offending lords were marched into the room. The charge against them was an outrage on the king and queen, tending to a breach of the public peace. No defence was offered, and the prisoners were both condemned. Here the king stepped in. Justice had said her say: Mercy was ready with her healing voice. The two offenders, he declared, were in the wrong, for they had sinned against the law; but kings are full of grace, and he, as sovereign, was prepared to take a lenient course. He wished his servants to be friends. Would they forgive each other? He desired to be a peace-maker. If they would forgive each other, he, their prince, would overlook their faults, and be a means to get their pardon from the queen. Her majesty was angry, as she had good right to be; but he would go to her, and take the matter on himself. He begged, he wept. A king in tears was such a sight as no man then alive had seen. Grey melted at the sight. What mattered it to him how such a braggart as Southampton lied? In answer to the king's appeal, he held his hand out to his foe. James wept still more for joy than he had done for grief. Peace in his household was restored.

It was a spurious peace—a foretaste of the still more spurious peace to come.

Twelve days after that scene in the council-chamber, Grey was committed to the Tower. Raleigh soon followed Grey.

One day the Founder of Free States was standing on the Terrace, waiting for his majesty, who was expected to come out by the Private stair with whip and pack. Above him rose the gallery in which he had knelt to his great mistress, when he first unveiled to her his plan of founding in her name an Empire in the West. Those labours filled his heart; but they were only to be carried forward by a prince who was prepared to stand across the path of Spain. As yet, the king had not pronounced his final word. Each side was courting him; here, the Catholic powers —there, the Evangelical League. No one was sure which way his face might turn. Vere was still holding out; Nottingham held the fleet in readiness; Cobham was busy at the Cinque Ports. In spite of his apparent leaning towards the Spaniards, there were grounds for hope that James might take the better side. Anne was in favour of a liberal policy; Christiern was known to have urged his brother-in-law to act on Raleigh's advice; Raleigh had put his thoughts into writing; and had sent that writing to the king: giving him a perfect picture of the state of Spain, and showing him how easily her fleets might be driven from the sea. If James would only hear the truth, king and people might be reconciled, the imperial squadrons might be swept from the Channel, and a group of English colonies might be planted in the West.

But James had no heart for such heroic deeds. He yearned for peace with Spain. To him, Spain was Southampton multiplied by millions. She could set the Jesuits on him; she could raise the kernes against him. Spain had agencies in every house; many such agencies, male and female, in his own. Lady Suffolk was for Spain; Lady Rich and Lady Derby were for Spain; the catholics in his ante-room were all for Spain. And in his heart he was himself for Spain.

Raleigh, though hoping against hope, had many on his side. The queen and prince thought as he thought. The admirals and captains of Elizabeth were all for fighting out the fight. Bacon was with him ; Vere and Nottingham were with him. Shakespere, freed from his bondage to Southampton, stood with his independent countrymen. That war with Spain was not a quarrel to be ended by a compromise. It was a war of principle, in which the English people were contending for advantages more precious than their lives—the freedom of their country, the existence of their church. On sea and land that battle had been fought for five-and-twenty years. Could any man pretend the victory had yet been won ? The enemy was not only in the field, but in the Channel. He had gained possession, not alone of Antwerp, but the Scheldt. His armies were encamped before Ostend. That fortress carried, Spain would become a Channel power. Was that a time to prate of peace with Austro-Spain ?

To peace as peace, no one objected ; but the wiser sort desired to win a solid peace, not to purchase a deceitful truce. Shakespere expressed the general thought:

'Heaven grant us its peace, but not the King of Hungary's.'

Agents of Rudolf of Austria, 'King of Hungary,' were at work in Lady Suffolk's closet and in Lady Rich's drawing-room, offering such terms of peace as would have laid the country at Cæsar's feet. Lady Suffolk and Lady Rich, weighted with doubloons, were all for peace—even though it had to be the King of Hungary's peace.

Raleigh waited on the Terrace, but no king came out. After a time, Cecil crept down the Private stair, and saluted Raleigh with the message: 'I come from the king.' Cecil asked the sailor to go up into the king's cabinet. Some matters had been opened to the lords in which his name appeared. The king desired him to explain. Raleigh went up into the cabinet, where he heard to his astonishment that he was charged with a conspiracy to support the king of Spain !

Proudly he pointed to his course of life, and to the writings he had lately laid before the king. He pointed to his protests and his arguments against the peace. James heard him, and adjourned the council; but a few days afterwards the state-founder was conveyed to the Tower—a sacrifice to his intended policy in Madrid.

Vere was removed; Ostend allowed to fall. Fresh agents from the Emperor and the King of Spain arrived. These agents of corruption plied their trade, and when the male and female favourites had been pensioned off, his majesty signed the articles of his spurious peace.

Before he quitted Windsor, James had shown his mind, and raised suspicion of his aim and policy in the heart of every man who was neither slave of Rome nor pensioner of Spain. The people were disgusted, but the sectaries, sniffing the coming fight, waxed warmer in their zeal:—a Papist court might call into being an Anabaptist camp.

CHAPTER VI.

KING CHRISTIERN.

1606–14.

If any man were likely to arrest the Stuarts on their downward course, he was the powder-loving Dane. Christiern came over twice; each time in the belief that James, disgusted by the failure of his Spanish policy, might be induced to take a straighter course, and win the people over whom he reigned by going for the English cause.

The first time was in 1606, a few months after the Powder Plot. That scheme had proved the folly of taking fribbles like Southampton as security against the Jesuits and their slaves. Rome might be moderate, but she had agents in England who would not hear of peace, except on terms dictated by themselves. In spite of the many favours shown to catholics, these agents laid their curse on every one who took an oath of

fealty to the king. They said they were deceived
in James. A catholic by birth, by baptism, and
by early training, he had still not proved himself
catholic enough for them. They wanted to be all
in all—to rule the land as they had ruled it under
Cardinal Pole. At Holyrood, surrounded by conventicles, they had permitted James to hide his
faith; but here, in Windsor, in the sanctuary of
St. George, they expected him to show his loyalty to
the catholic church. The country, they declared,
was catholic, and likely to be more submissive to
a catholic prince than to a heretic. So long as
he denied his church, he must not hope for grace,
nor must good catholics obey him as a lawful
king.

James put out a pamphlet on the Oath of
Allegiance; but the Papal agents, knowing their
man as well as the Scottish laddies knew him,
treated him and his with scorn. Christiern supposed that even James's craven spirit must revolt
at last; and under that belief he crossed the sea
and came to lodge on the royal mount.

A crisis had arrived in Italy which opened out
new prospects for the Evangelical League. Paolo
the Fifth had laid an interdict on Venice, and the
doge, Donato, was up in arms. This rupture was

dividing Europe on a novel set of lines. The Evangelical States were all for Venice; the Catholic States were nearly all for Rome. Here, lay a chance, as Christiern thought, for England to step in.

No foreign city had so many charms for English folks as Venice. In her water-lanes, under her marble domes, and on her sunny piazzas, English travellers were at home. The strength, the beauty, the repose of Venice, took all hearts. The poets sought in her materials for the stage. She was a witchery and a problem; hardly more attractive in the gaiety of her quays, than in the bustle of her arsenals and the mystery of her courts. She wrought on the imagination like a spell. Shakespere, who never went to Spain for a subject, turned again and again to Venice and her inland cities, Padua and Verona. Not to have seen Venice was to have seen nothing; and to die without having crossed the Rialto and saluted the Giant's Stair, was to die without having lived. Even to the untravelled man, the city of Shylock and Othello was no foreign place. The words Rialto and Piazza dropped on the public ear like those of London Bridge and Paul's Cross. Yet Venice was not better known as a seat of song than as a refuge; as a town in which the Jew and Moor, scorched out of Spain and Sicily by Inquisitors, were allowed to live. Monks said mass in San Marco; convents covered the lagunes from Mala-mocco to Murano; yet the republic had given more trouble to Rome than either England or Germany. On her lagunes, the strife with Rome had taken the ferocious aspect of a civil war. Free from bigotry, the mariners, silversmiths, and printers of Venice, though holding on to the creeds and rituals of Rome, had never crouched with Celtic terror at her voice; nor had they suffered her canonists and cardinals to override their local laws. Some sense of rivalry had tended to divide the two cities, each of which aspired to be the capital of the world: one through her doctrines, her confessionals, and her religious orders; the other, through her literature, her com-merce, and her fleets. Rome had steeled her-self against Venice; Venice had armed herself against Rome. The mariners and silversmiths were alarmed by what appeared to them the revival of an 'age of faith;' an age in which the monks might want to rule, and laymen might be driven to fight for their invaded rights. To guard their liberties, they renewed two ancient laws against the clergy. One of these laws provided that no new church or chapel should be opened in their States without the express consent of doge and council; and the second law declared that any death-bed legacy to church or cloister should be considered null and void. Paolo the Fifth, egged on by Spain, required the doge to cancel these obnoxious laws as insults to the Holy See. Fuel was heaped on fire by the arrest of two ecclesiastics by the civil power. Even in the land of the 'Decameron,' the crimes of these holy men were startling. A canon of Vicenza broke the seals of his chancery and outraged the person of a lady of his blood; an abbot of Nervasa killed his father, violated his sister, and poisoned some of his monks. Paolo denounced the civil courts for daring to lay hands on these offenders. Sarpi, the most eloquent preacher of his generation, sided with the doge—upholding the civil law against his church. Paolo, launching an interdict at Venice, called on emperor, kings, and dukes, to execute his curse.

Donato looked around for allies. Wotton was then English agent near the doge. A poet and a scholar, he threw his soul into her fight. All English people, save the partisans of Spain, went with him. In the House of Commons, money-bills were voted with a view to raising troops and arming vessels for the war. James was persuaded that his own pamphlet on the Oath of Allegiance had stirred the Signiory into an assertion of their independence. Carried forward by the flood, he knighted Molino, the Venetian agent, and accepted the doge's scheme for a defensive league.

Christiern came to Windsor, in the hope of setting James in the right way to help the liberal cause.

At first he prospered in his course. 'Turn back, begin afresh,' was his advice. 'Distrust the catholics, who surround you only to betray you; drive away the Jesuits; tender the Oath of Allegiance; unmask your enemies; receive the doge's envoy into greater favour, and dismiss the Suffolk family from your court.'

So far, James was driven along by his impetuous brother-in-law. The Jesuits were put on board, the oaths were tendered, and those who refused to swear were either fined or sent to jail. Suffolk and his wife were driven from court; Molino came to Windsor, where the king, in Christiern's presence, bade him tell the doge and Signiory that their cause was good, and they might count on him for help by sea and land.

Yet when the Dane, elated by success, reminded

James that his new policy implied new council-lors, the king fell back. Christiern, like the queen, his sister, and his nephew, Henry, turned towards Raleigh's dungeon in the Tower. When anything great was to be done, Raleigh was always in their thoughts. If Venice was to be sustained, Raleigh must be called to council, and the Lennoxes and Southamptons pushed aside. James shrank from this advice, and Christiern soon perceived that he was wasting time. After more whisky had been drunk, more powder burnt, he left the Thames, convinced that, whether Venice sank or swam, no English squadron would be sent to sea.

Eight years later he came again, still hoping against hope. Another crisis had arrived, and this time, nearer home. Henry, the gallant prince, was dead, and Charles, his ricketty younger brother, was now heir-apparent. Elizabeth, their sister, married to Friedrich, Palatine of the Rhine, had gone to Heidelberg. Cecil was dead ; Suffolk and Southampton were the leading councillors. The highest offices at court were filled by catholics, and men who were catholic in everything but the name, were solidly entrenched within the church. The time had come for some one to step in. Friedrich, the king's son-in-law, was president of the Evangelical Union, and the object of attack to every member of the Catholic League. The powers were all afield, and any day the first shot might be fired — the opening passage of a great religious war.

A crowd of English volunteers was on the Rhine, all serving on the protestant side. The councillors at Westminster and Windsor were supposed to favour the catholic cause. Christiern imagined that his presence might induce the king to go with his people, not against them; the more so, since his daughter's province was at stake.

Meaning to surprise the king, and score his point before the enemy guessed his game, he left for Elsinore, where he talked of going to see his friends, the German dukes, and sent his servants to a Baltic port, with orders to await his coming. When the men were gone, he chose three vessels, and attended by a few guards and trumpeters, he walked on board, and gave the signal for that Baltic port. At sea he changed his course and made for Yarmouth, where he landed in disguise, hired horses, rode to Aldgate, dined at a common tavern, stepped into a street cab, and drove to Somerset House. The king was out of town; but Anne, his sister was at home, just sitting down to dine when he alighted at the gate. Cardel, a French dancer, who had seen him eight years before at Windsor, ran to tell the queen her brother had arrived. Anne laughed at him, and went on eating, saying it was all illusion—a 'French caprice.' Christiern, close on his heels, waved the attendants into silence, crept behind his sister, caught her in his arms, and kissed her merrily. Anne snatched a jewel from her bosom, which she flung to the dancer for his news, sent off fast riders to announce her brother's coming to the king, and then sat down again to dinner with her guest.

A panic spread among the pensioners of Spain. Why had he come over, and with so much secresy? Shrewd minds suspected that the German business was in hand. Great hopes were raised, great fears excited, by his presence. All that the catholics had won seemed put in jeopardy. But James, though willing to write letters of remonstrance, was unwilling to draw the sword. In truth, he was expected to obtain a catholic consort for his son. A week in England satisfied the Dane that James would never fire a shot, never disturb ' the King of Hungary's peace.' By way of Parthian bolt, he gave a sword and one of his men-of-war to his nephew Charles.

Worse things soon came : the rout of Prague ; the fall of Friedrich ; the exile of the Queen of Hearts ; but Christiern made no more attempts to check the Stuarts in their downward course.

CHAPTER VII.

A CATHOLIC DEAN.

1618.

ONE step in that downward course was the bringing into Windsor of a Catholic dean.

This singular personage was Marco Antonio, archbishop of Spalatro, whom the king and his advisers, yearning after the things of Rome, induced to visit England, to accept the deanery, and to settle on the royal mount.

Spalatro was a corsair port on the Dalmatian coast. Ruins of an old palace covered more than half the town; a maze of sinks and alleys, tenanted by pirates, fishwives, polenta-cooks, and bare-legged friars. Chapels and cloisters overlooked the mole; but the main building was a temple of Jupiter, a pile too solid for the robbers to haul down. Dirty and decayed, Spalatro was about the poorest see in the papal world. Once, indeed, she had claimed a primacy; but the bishops of Venice had long since filched away her clerical rank. No state, and not much revenue, was left. Except in name, a parish priest in Venice was of greater might than his grace of Spalatro. But the name was much, at least in the eyes of people in a distant country and of a different creed. Marco found in his name a talisman strong enough to carry him from his pirate lair into the deanery of Windsor and the registry of St. George.

At fifty-one, when he first came to England, Marco was fat and gross, with swarthy skin, dark eyes, bull-neck, and sensual mouth. Dressed in his Dalmatian robe, he had a striking and out-landish air. Few understood his words, but every one observed his cap and gown. He spoke no English, and his Latin was a barbarous dialect. Learning he had next to none; not a single word of Hebrew, hardly a single scrap of Greek. Even in the Scriptures he was very much at fault. What he knew best was science, but his studies in the school of Galileo had been faint and few. An Oriental, he was showy, voluble, self-indulgent; fond of things not found in a pirate port—soft bed and ample board, rich hangings, troops of ser-

vants, smiles of high-born women, and companion-
ship of kings and princes. All these comforts
he had learned were to be found at Windsor,
and to Windsor he had come—invited by the
king.

Who was this Oriental priest?

Born at Arba, in the Gulf of Venice, Marco
Antonio de Dominis was a subject of the doge:
one of those 'provincials,' who supplied Venetian
comedy with buts and dupes. In seeking bread
he had become a monk. Being glib of tongue,
he had won the notice of some Jesuit fathers, who
imagined they could train him for the preacher's
stand and the professor's chair. The story-tellers
of his country had a gift of rolling out floods of
talk. Marco inherited that gift. Adopted by the
Jesuit order, he had been put to school; first in
Loreto, afterwards in Padua; where he had dawdled
through his classes, but had picked up little by the
way. On finishing his course, he had been set to
teach and preach. All theories were one to him:
science, rhetoric, divinity; on each and all he was
prepared to roll out floods of words. Years had
gone by without results, until the fathers, finding
their empty dream a failure, had shelved him on
his native coast, as bishop of Segna; one of a group

of pirate ports, in which no decent pastor cared to risk his life.

There, for a time, he had droned his services and shared the spoil of his unruly flock. But he and his penitents had; fallen into strife. A cruiser, lying off the roads, had tempted him with sequins to betray some members of his fold to justice ; but the robbers being caught and hung, some of their kinsmen threatened ' to make a bag of his skin,' like the pigskin bags in which they kept their wine. Not waiting to be peeled and cured, Marco had taken boat, landed on the Piazzetta, and claimed protection from the doge.

At Venice, a wider field had opened on his view. Venice and Rome were fighting in that quarrel which had called out Sarpi, and brought the royal Dane to Windsor. Luckier than Christiern, he had made his game of that affair. Having managed to convince the doge that he was all for Venice, and the Pope that he was all for Rome, Donato and Paolo the Fifth agreed in sending him to Spalatro as archbishop. To Spalatro he had gone, with what he held to be two pledges : Rome having secretly engaged to restore that primacy to his see which Venice had usurped, and Venice having secretly engaged to protect him against intrigues in Rome.

But he had no more liking to his second pirates than his first. Ready to seek his blessings, the Spalatriotes had been slow to pay his dimes. He had been forced to wink at piracy, and when times were dull, to shut his eyes on differences in the flag. Crescents were held to be lawful spoil, but when the flags of Venice and Ancona began to strew the mole, warnings had come in from many sides. Rome, instead of sending him his bull of primacy, had instructed her agents to dog his steps, to note his teaching, and report on his ways of life. Disgusted by such treatment, he had fled once more to the lagunes, where he supposed his presence and his oratory would provoke new storms between the Church and State. But he had found the situation changed. Venice and Rome had long ago come to terms. Loud voices and rush of words no longer roused the doge and Signiory to arms. His business as disturber of the peace had died a natural death.

How came this broken priest to Windsor — to the lodgings of an English dean?

Just as he was sinking under public odium, Marco had met an English clergyman, who gave a new direction to his thoughts. Bedell, chaplain of the English embassy in Venice, was a man of simple heart, with high-church sentiments, and a child-like ignorance of the world. In Marco, he beheld a Roman dignitary—bishop, archbishop, primate. Of his life at Segna and Spalatro, he knew nothing. What he saw before him was a man of apostolic grace, in whom the ordination was complete and sure. Marco had made much of him, and he of Marco. In a week they had become intimate; Marco the father, Bedell his obedient son. Marco had asked about the state of English bishops and primates. With a pardonable pride, his ' son ' had described their rank and power, their palaces and revenues. Fresh from a dinner of sprats and polenta, how, with other than a yearning heart, could Marco hear of prelates who sat by the side of kings, and squandered incomes greater than a doge? No further proof was needed; such a church, he had felt assured, must be the church of Christ. Could he exchange into that church?

On Bedell reminding him that England had renounced her connexion with the see of Rome, he had replied that he was ready to renounce his own connexion with that see. Rome had become, he said, corrupt in morals and unsound in faith.

She had betrayed her trust, and forfeited her primacy in the church. On Bedell asking whether he had put these views into writing, he had answered, No; but he was ready to begin. As a Venetian, he had always been opposed to Rome. Then, day by day, he had sent in sheets on sheets of manuscript for his son to read. Bedell, surprised to find so many of his facts mis-stated, so many of his references wrong, so many of his quotations made at second hand, was driven to make excuses for his friend. The motives were so good that he had been content to overskip the faults. If emperors may be above grammar, why not primates? Mending what was faulty, Bedell had put the facts into order, purged the arguments, and supplied the references. On getting back his manuscripts, Marco had chuckled:—'I can do nothing without Bedell.'

The chaplain won, Marco had advanced a step. Would Bedell speak for him to the ambassador? Marco had a strong desire to see the king, whose tractate on the Oath of Allegiance, he declared, had opened his eyes to the unjust pretensions of the Holy See. Carleton, the ambassador, might procure an invitation for him to visit James. Carleton, seeing his drift, had told Bedell to ask him how

much money he would want. 'How much?' the
holy man had sighed. Well, pomp and state were
not for him: he wanted nothing but to find his
rest in the true church; still, he was waxing old,
and might require a man to help him in his cell.
Pressed to name a sum that would 'content him,'
he had answered that he should count two hundred
pounds a-year as 'a good estate.'

Laud and other romanizers easily persuaded
James to ask the venerable prelate to his court.
Marco started for the north, in secresy; concealing
his intentions from the catholic powers. When
he was near the Straits, the question rose of how
and where he should be lodged. Laud suggested
Lambeth palace. Abbot objected. He-disliked the
business, even before he saw the man. 'Let those
who want Spalatro pay for him,' he answered; but
the king entreated him to receive the venerable
man. He yielded, so far, as to say that he would
house and feed him, till some better lodging could
be found.

Strange stories came with him from Venice;
stories of pirates, jesuits, and seraglios; but the
king received him with respect; Villiers listened
to his floods of speech, Laud knelt to him as a
man of apostolic grace. Williams feasted him;

and after ransacking the Italian shops, discovered that his guest preferred Windsor venison to their Venetian cates.

Abbot soon sickened of his burly inmate; who, in turn, complained to James that he was lodged with a man who left him to starve. James offered him the deanery of Windsor and the registry of St. George—posts in which he would be as near the court. By adding the rectory of West Ildsley and the mastership of the Savoy, his majesty raised the 'estate' to eight hundred pounds a-year, with three good houses. On these pleasant terms Marco, fugitive from Spalatro, came to Windsor; came in the month of May, when fruit-trees are in blossom, and the gardens of the deanery are ablaze with flowers. Opening his lattice on the wall, he saw a vision of repose and plenty, that was to be recalled, when, at the end of his strange career, he lay in his dungeon of St. Angelo, dying at the feet of his indignant Pope.

CHAPTER VIII.

APOSTASY.

1619–22.

'You don't yet know your dean,' said Gondomar to the king in one of his cynical bursts; 'he is a papist; he will cheat you of your money, and then betray you to the Pope.'

'He has renounced the Pope,' objected James.

'In words, only in words; your majesty will see,' replied the Spanish count.

Some people smiled, more people snarled, at the introduction of this foreign dean. No living man had seen a Romish priest at Windsor. Since the college was erected, not a single alien had occupied the president's chair; St. George of Windsor was St. George of England; never until now had he been served by foreign dean. Why was this alien introduced by James?

Whispers ran abroad that Marco was a jesuit,

that his apostasy was a sham, and that his secret object was to reconcile the king and introduce the Pope. Suspicion walked with him on the slope and followed him to the King's house. Such men as Morton, King, and Neyle distrusted him from the first, while others waited for him to disclose his game. They listened to his homilies with a puzzled air; for while he tore the Pope to rags and tatters, he evinced no knowledge of the principles in dispute. So far as he preached anything, beyond abuse of Paolo the Fifth, he preached the dogmas which all reformers, from Cranmer to Calvin, had renounced. His creed was nothing but a burning rage against the Pope; a thing for which no Knight of the Garter and no burgess of Windsor cared one rush. They were in arms against the papacy, not against the Pope; he was in arms against the Pope and not against the papacy. Bacon and Andrewes went to hear him preach. 'Is he a Protestant?' asked the philosopher. 'I know not,' answered the divine, 'if he is a Protestant, but I think he is a Detestant.' Marco's hatred of the Pope was overdone, and many of his auditors believed him to be playing a comedy arranged for him in Rome.

Apart from what he preached, he wrapped himself in a Romish garb. Though lodged in the dean's house, he refused to take the name of dean. Though naturalised in England, he retained his foreign titles, and expected councillors and bishops to address him as 'your grace.' While taking English pay as rector, dean, and master, he affected to remain a dignitary of the Roman church.

Four years this personage reigned at Windsor; sitting near the king, and acting as his councillor in church affairs. Jealousies beset him from the first, and as he came to show his greed, these jealousies kindled into rage. As he annoyed the few who understood his words, he outraged the many who suffered from his acts.

In passing from Venice to Windsor, he had brought with him the habits of a corsair port; and much as he had sheared his flock at Segna and Spalatro, he proposed to fleece his tenantry in Bucks and Berks. Why should he not? As dean he had a right to his dues—all that his college property could be made to yield. In spite of warnings, he raised the rents, ousted the tenants from their farms, and sold reversions of house and land. Under him the college glebes were treated like the spoil of a piratical raid, of which the pastor claimed to have the lion's share. Scandals arose. Some of his canons spoke to him. His way, they said, was not an English way; their chapter was a pious body, trying to do good, and set a pattern for knight and squire, not a trading company, intent on wringing the last penny from the soil. No tenant coming to renew his lease had ever been answered in fee and fine. Their property was a model of the Christian commonwealth. Marco laughed. Model or no model, he must have his dues; and in his greed he turned adrift old tenants, who had held their farmsteads longer than the oldest canon in the college had enjoyed his stall.

Swarms of enemies were made in Berks and Bucks; yet Marco kept his deanery and his other livings in the church. He was a necessary man.

James liked him. King and dean had much in common. Born in the same year, they had lived through similar events; bred in poor countries, they had known the want of money; sprinkled into the same church, they had each strayed from the flock, without finally separating from the fold. Each thought himself an eloquent and learned man. Each spoke a copious dialect, hardly understood by strangers. Each believed he had been chosen to effect a miracle—the reconciliation of two hostile creeds.

Marco perceived that James was trying to front two ways, one eye resting on Lambeth, where his secular kingdom lay, another eye on Rome, where he imagined that his spiritual kingdom lay. James, he observed, was willing to address the Pope as 'holy father,' and admit his primacy in the Western Church. So far as he dared to go, he was inclined to go; not only for the sake of Rome, but for the sake of Spain. Against the wishes of his people, he was seeking in Madrid a consort for his son. If Rome were only gained, he saw no reason why the families of Spain and England should not be one household, as they had been under Mary's reign, when Philip was grand master of St. George. The thought was natural, though unfortunate, in a son of Mary, queen of Scots.

Marco took ground between the king and Pope, as he had once between the doge and Pope, meaning to make his market out of each. Much as he had won the see of Spalatro, he expected to achieve the primacy of York.

In secresy, he opened out to James a scheme for reconciling the church of England to the church of Rome. Each side would yield a little, but not much; the two religions being on all essential articles the same. If each would give and take— a rule of discipline here, a point of doctrine there —the parties might shake hands. If both sides wished for peace, a way might easily be found. A way! He was himself the way. On his arrival more than half the work was done. He was the messenger and minister of grace. Up to that date, no ground of union had existed, since the papal courts had never recognised the English bishops as men ordained. Ambassadors cannot meet till they admit each other's powers. That obstacle was now removed. In him the English orders were restored.

Here lay, in fact, the work for which he had been brought to Windsor and invested with the deanery by James. The old fable of Parker's ordination at the Nag's Head, in Cheapside, had recently been revived by Fitzherbert, who asserted that the documents cited in Bramhall's answer to the charge, were forged. Abbot had shown the papers to four catholic priests, and offered them to public sight; but Laud, and men of his opinion, were not satisfied with proofs. Hating Elizabeth's bishops, they desired to have a new episcopacy, deriving their apostolate from a 'purer' source.

That source, in their belief, was only to be sought on papal soil. In Marco, archbishop of Spalatro, the divine succession was secured.

The work of founding a new bench of bishops was proceeding. Marco laid hands on Felton and Monteigne. These prelates were his 'sons,' and were supposed to have a higher share of grace. In turn, these pastors laid their hands on others. Fotherby, Tonson, Davenant, Williams, were of this order; which at length included Laud, and those on whom he laid his hands. Abbot and the sober prelates watched these efforts to replace the line of English bishops with dismay, as being a cause of strife. It cast a doubt on every thing that had been done for sixty years, and touched the people in the most private relations of their lives.

Marco, on his side, was displeased. No see was given to him in exchange for his apostolic grace. Salisbury, Lincoln, London, passed under his nose into meaner hands. His livings only yielded him a thousand pounds a-year. King, his diocesan, grudged him his Windsor dues, and hindered him from making the most of his estate. Only one member of his college, Canon Goodman, was converted to his doctrines; and this papist canon, to whom he made over his rectory of West

Ildsley, stood against him in the question of his fines and rents. A time was coming when he might need to fly from Windsor, as he had flown from Segna and Spalatro; and in view of that evil day, he scraped and saved, and locked up money in his trunks.

James heard with pain that Marco was not only screwing the last penny from his tenants, but proclaiming popery in St. George's chapel. 'He preaches purgatory,' one of the knights complained.

'He is a rogue,' sneered Gondomar, who happened to be standing by: 'a rogue who has cajoled your majesty's bishops from the first.'

But James stood up for his dean:

'He has abjured the papacy.'

'Sire, he is not only a papist, but a subject of the Pope.'

Knowing him to be a naturalised and beneficed subject, James held out.

'You doubt my word,' said Gondomar. 'Give me leave to confer with him, and I will bring you evidence of his being a papist and a follower of the Pope.'

James gave him leave to see the dean.

CHAPTER IX.

EXPULSION.

1621–2.

Waiting on the dean, Gondomar informed him, in a tone of sympathy, that his rival, Paolo the Fifth, had passed away, and that Gregory the Fifteenth had been chosen in his place. Marco, he knew, had been at school with Gregory, and he spoke of them adroitly as mates and friends. The new Pope, Gondomar assured him, wished to see his grace, and to have the benefit of his advice. If he returned to Rome, Gregory was prepared, not merely to receive him well, but to reward him with a cardinal's hat, and grant him a post worth twelve thousand crowns a-year.

The bait was gross, but not too gross for Marco's tooth. Twelve thousand crowns a-year! Glancing at his trunks, in which he had stowed away his plate and money, he weighed his poor savings at Windsor in the scale against twelve thousand crowns a-year. After all his scraping, he had only saved some seventeen hundred pounds in coin and three or four hundred pounds in plate. Twelve thousand Roman crowns made three thousand English pounds. One year in Rome was worth three years at Windsor. Then there was the cardinal's hat!

Was the ambassador sure? Yes, the ambassador was sure. That Gregory would forgive what he had said and done? Yes, all that he had said and done; for all that he had said and done, could easily be unsaid, undone.

What evidence had he to produce?

None in his hands; but he could bring it by return of post. What evidence would his grace prefer?

A pardon for his past offences, answered Marco, sealed with the Fisherman's Seal.

Gondomar pledged his word, that quickly as a messenger could go through Spain to Rome and back, he would produce that pardon from the Pope.

In due time he returned to Marco with the pardon, sealed with the leaden seal: 'You sign these papers, and the Holy See is yours—the cardinal's hat and the twelve thousand crowns a-year.'

Marco read the forms and signed. In one, he cancelled and disowned his writings on the church, and in the other he submitted to the Pope. A priest at variance with his chief could not expect a cardinal's hat. His peace was made, and he had only to set out for Rome. His passport would be sent to him on the road.

Taking up the papers, Gondomar went to court and begged an audience of the king.

'I told your majesty his grace of Spalatro was a papist and a follower of the Pope. Here are my proofs.'

Scared by this unmasking of his dean, the king's first impulse was to take such measures as would stop his tongue. For years he had been trusting Marco with his secrets; talking with him on the most dangerous of all topics—that of a return of England to the papal yoke. Yet this man was in private correspondence with the Pope; begging and accepting pardon from the Vatican, and proposing to set out for Rome! What had he said—what had he done?

To open correspondence with the papacy, without a royal warrant, was a public crime, indictable in the courts of law. But James, though angry with his dean, was most concerned about himself. Except a papist here and there, every man in England was disgusted by his murder of Raleigh, his desertion of the Queen of Hearts, and his projected match for Charles. If James was known to have been treating with the Pope, nobody would be bold enough to answer for the public peace. Aware of what he had been saying to Marco on that point, he shuddered lest the dean should blab, and thought of sealing his lips by lodging him in gaol.

But such a course, his councillors felt, was equally uncertain and unsafe. Suspicious people would declare that he was silenced lest his words should compromise the king. Cæsar was likely to object; his holiness was certain to object. If Gregory required the prisoner at his hands, what could he say? The application would be backed by all the catholic powers. On second thoughts, a milder course was taken; that of trying to frighten and cajole the dean. No one knew, as yet, what he had said in Rome—in whose name he had spoken—if he had talked of having power to treat. One point, at least, was clear—he, and he only, could remove suspicion and discharge the king of blame. Could he be either frightened or cajoled into signing a statement that no single word had passed between the king and him about reunion with the Roman see?

Taking this milder course, they waited for the dean to move. At length, he asked permission to retire; alleging that the air of Windsor was too cold for him—that the pontiff wished him to return—and that, in his new position, he hoped 'to work the inward peace and tranquillity' of the realm. Monteigne, his 'son,' and Neyle, his critic, went to him. Telling him they came from the king, Neyle asked how he was holding intercourse with Rome unknown to his majesty, and what he meant by 'making the inward peace' of England? Taken by surprise, he owned that he had no letter from the Pope; only some letters from his friends. Asked to produce these letters, he pretended he had burnt them. By his working 'the inward peace,' he said, he meant that he would get the Pope to tolerate the oaths. 'But that alone will hardly serve for peace,' objected Neyle. 'There are twelve hours in the day,' replied the dean, 'and I must leave the rest to God.'

Neyle pressed him hard. How could he be a member of the church of England and the church of Rome? Marco thought he could. Take an example, answered Neyle; England denies the real presence in the bread and wine; Rome affirms that presence in the bread and wine. Marco replied that both were true. 'But I have heard you say, you never did, and never could, believe in Transubstantiation,' Neyle exclaimed. 'Yes, my lord, I have said so, and I say so still; but that can be explained away on philosophical grounds.'

Driven into a corner, Marco doffed his cap, and made a declaration, that in his belief the church of England was a true and orthodox church.

The services of Morton were employed. It was essential that the dean should sign a statement freeing the king from blame; and Marco being a timid man, the council thought he could be frightened into doing what they wished. Naturalised and beneficed, he was subject to the law. To correspond with Rome, in view of bringing back the Pope, was treason, and the penalty of that offence was death. Marco, a subject, had incurred that penalty, and nothing but royal grace could save him from the block. Startled by this announcement, Marco asked to see the king. James refused to give him audience. He must sign the paper; but a hope was held out, that after he had signed, he would be suffered to resign his offices, renounce his citizenship, and leave the kingdom with his trunks. He stood between two fires. At Windsor he was subject to the law ; at Rome he would be subject to the inquisition. Where was he to find a form of words to satisfy James without offending Gregory? To Morton's questions, he replied that he had dreamt of union, because he found the church of England very much like the church of Rome.

'Your grace proposes to convert the Pope and cardinals ?'

'Why not, my lord,' retorted Marco; 'do you count them as devils, lying beyond the reach of grace ?'

'No, I by no means count them devils; neither do I consider his grace of Spalatro to be God, and able to effect a miracle.'

Shuffling to the last, he tried to steal away, without committing his pen so far as to vex the Pope and jeopardise his cardinal's hat. But officers of the council watched him by day and night. They left him free to go about, but always in a ring of fire. Taking a boat, he dropt to Greenwich, where he hired a lodging by the water-side, and got a ketch in readiness to sail. This done, he packed his trunks, and was about to move them, when his watch appeared. 'Nothing could be moved,' said the officer on duty; 'empty you came in, empty you go out.' To leave his plate and money—all that he had rasped and saved at Windsor—was too much for Marco. But the nets were tightening round him every day. His rents and fines were stopt. His offers to resign the deanery were rejected, yet his salary was withheld. In no long time he might be short of bread. Whither could he look for help? Gondomar no longer came to him. Abbot was his enemy. Carleton, once his friend, was now disgusted by his greed. His 'son' was silenced and abashed. In his despair he went to Gondomar, who repulsed him with contempt and violence:

'Begone, and trouble me no more! I have unmasked you to the king. Do what you like. Stay here—and starve. Go back—and burn. That is your choice. Get out, I have done with you!'

Baffled on every side, he yielded to the council, signed what he was told to sign, and got a license to resign his deanery and renounce his citizenship. He hoped to get a license to depart in peace and honour—with his trunks; but Gondomar urged the king to brand him with discredit, and expel him by a public act. James leapt at the idea. Marco, once beyond the sea, was sure to blab, and it seemed wise to cover him beforehand by a cloud of shame. His tales, regarded as revenge, would have less weight in foreign courts. At home, where he was hated with unusual warmth, a sentence of expulsion would be well received.

Abbot, assisted by Mandeville and other commissioners, called him up, exposed his dealings and apostasies, refused him a license to quit the realm, and sentenced him to an expulsion within twenty days—never to come back on peril of his life.

Gondomar thanked his majesty for having rid his kingdom of such a rogue.

A few months later, Sackville called to see him in the castle of St. Angelo. 'My lord of Spalatro,' said the Englishman, 'you have here a dark lodging. It was not so with you in England. There, you had, at Windsor, as good a prospect by land as was in all the country, and at the Savoy, you had the best prospect by water as was in all the city.'

Marco looked up at his prison-wall, and sighed:

'I have forgot those things. Here I can best contemplate the kingdom of heaven.'

Sackville, going into another room, turned to the rector:

'Do you think this man is employed in the contemplation of heaven?'

'He was a malcontent knave,' replied the rector, 'when he fled from us; a railing knave while he lived with you; and a parti-coloured knave now he has come again.'

Marco kissed the crucifix and died; using these words:

'I die a member of the Roman Catholic church.'

So passed away the jesuit dean of Windsor—leaving his policy to Goodman, his apostolate to Laud.

CHAPTER X.

FOREST RIGHTS.

1621–5.

A BLISTER on the town and country was that Stuart policy of closing the royal parks; a blister bringing to a head all evil humours in the body politic. Cranbourne Chase and the royal forest had been closed soon after the Little park. Men's minds were turned against the king, and yet his conies and his billets were not saved. No longer gathered by the poor in open day, his sticks were filched by poachers' wives at night. Intruders of a lower class made war on his preserves. Where Page and Ford had stalked through his grass with dog and gun, Pistol and Patrico now laid their wires, while Prue o' the Park and Long Meg of Eton gathered up the lops and tops.

Bad blood grew up between town and Castle; for the burgesses, though hardly caring to defend the poachers, showed by their silence that they thought the king's advisers were to blame. Year after year, the bickering of court and town waxed warmer. Why, asked the king pettishly, were those poachers allowed to snare his game, those doxies to steal his wood? Why, when he strove to check these injuries, had he found no help from the local magistrates? Were the townsmen at his Castle-gates inclined to cross his will, and drive him to some other house?

Opinion in the town and country ran so high, that mayors and aldermen were unable to enforce his rules. The parks and forests were regarded by his people as public lands, in which all the inhabitants had some common rights. James thought these parks and forests were his own— his own to shut or open when he liked, as freely as he shut and opened the door of his private room. No man in Windsor shared that view. The upper classes stood aloof, leaving the king's officers to deal with Patrico and Prue; yet not a little of their sympathy went in secret to those lawless challengers of the public right. They held their tongues, but help in putting down the mischief they had none to give. Among the lower classes, every voice was up for Patrico and Prue.

Lads, known to have smashed the king's fences, were the heroes of every ale-house porch.

'My sport! my sport!' groaned James; 'a king must have his sport.'

A state of mind arose at Windsor, and in other places, under which 'serious' persons raised the question whether sport was not a wicked thing. They saw the bad side plainly; and the good side, seen by their fathers, had been turned away. 'The king loves sport; the king is wicked; therefore, sport is wicked,' was a piece of reasoning constantly repeated, which the simplest mind could follow out. In time, these 'serious' persons set their teeth against sport, rejecting a round of pleasant things—plays, races, dances, masques, may-poles, and Christmas ales. Some of these 'serious' persons ceased to hunt and shoot. Sectaries, like Browne, drew converts from the 'better sort.' Justice put on a sterner face; and fines were levied in the town on men who followed the royal pastimes of oaths and drink. Shrewd people noted, as a portent, that a moral town was rising up against an immoral court. Most of the amusements in the King's house—revels, balls, and masques—fell under popular ban. Court ladies danced too late, court gentlemen drank too deep, the censors said. The masques were no less filthy than profane.

Pestered by these civic judges, James called in Ben Jonson to avenge him on the mayor and burgesses.

Jonson, a client of Lennox, had as much of the royal favour as a poet could expect. Much of what was best in Jonson was entirely lost on James; but Ben had crudities of mind, which, in his baser moments, lowered him to the royal plane. He was extremely fond of drink; he was inordinately foul of tongue; in sycophancy he knew no depth; no sense of religion guided his erratic steps. With James and Marco, he believed the church of England and the church of Rome were very much alike. Born a Calvinist, he had become a catholic. After the Powder Plot he had joined the court religion, and helped in hunting down his colleagues. James had made him Laureate, and he had to earn his hundred marks. If flattery were wanted, he was rich in phrases; if abuse were wanted, he was no less rank in venom. Both were needed by the king; flattery the most fulsome, abuse the most scurrilous, that poet had ever penned. In Jonson's Masque of the Gipsies, they were poured out to his full content.

This filthy piece was played by courtiers on the Windsor stage in James's presence. Jonson brought in mayor and burgesses, under the names of Townhead, Clod, Puppy, and 'other clowns,' with all the male and female riff-raff of the neighbourhood. They crawl into the royal ward to see how court ladies and gentlemen behave. They find a dance going on —a dance of gipsies, under their leaders, Patrico and Jackman. Patrico, seeing the mayor and burgesses, begins to patter:

> 'Why this is a sport,
>   See it north, see it south,
> For a taste of the court,
>   For the court's own mouth.'

Jackman, his pal, responds:

> 'Come Windsor the town,
>   With the mayor, and oppose
> We'll put them all down!'

Acting as chorus, Patrico sings:

> 'Do—do—down, like my hose!'

Next skip in the drabs and doxies of the town; Prue o' the Park, Frances o' the Castle, Long Meg of Eton, Peg o' the Dairy, and their sisters of the market-cross and the tavern yard. Mayor and burgesses get hustled; gipsies tell their fortunes, pick their pockets, and sing them nasty songs, at which they smack their lips like a set of canting rogues. A coarse rhyme and a free dance convert these Puritans into king's men, true lieges, and defenders of the royal sports. Gipsies and Puritans laud the king, first in his five senses separately, next in his virtues, taken as a whole :

> ' Bless him, too, from all offences,
> In his sports as in his senses,
> From a boy to cross his way,
> From a fall, or a foul day !
> Bless him, O bless him, heaven, and lend him long
> To be the sacred burden of all song.'

These imbecilities, for which Jonson got a reversion of the Revels and an offer of knighthood, were the only answers given by James to the mayor and burgesses who opposed his policy of returning to the Feudal times.

A year before his death, when coursing in the Moat park with Charles and Buckingham, the mayor, John Wickes, two aldermen, a country justice, and other gentlemen ' intruded ' on his sports. With these gentlemen came John Martin, vicar of Windsor, a man of moderate opinion, who was held by his parishioners in great respect. James had no patience with his moderate views.

The vicar preached against candle and crucifix, stole and altar-cloth—offences not to be overlooked by Marco's patron and Mary's son.

Coming up with the coursing party, Wickes presented a petition to the king:

' Eh, what about? '

It was about the vicar and the vicarage.

The church at Windsor had a poor endowment, which was almost swallowed up in rates. No man could live on the residue, yet the charge was not a small one ; since the town, governed by the new religious movement, counted more than a hundred communicants. Mayor and magistrates prayed the king, in his bounty, to increase the vicar's income by a canonry in his chapel of St. George.

Confer a canonry on the pastor of a church attended by Townhead, Puppy, and other clowns! James burned into sullen wrath. All through his reign he had been trying to turn his college of St. George into a nest of catholics. Install a man within his sanctuary who railed at altar-cloths ! He would do nothing of the kind. By doing so, he was assured that he would greatly please the burgesses. Please the burgesses ! What had the burgesses done that he should try to please them? Turning on Wickes, he stormed :

' Am I an ill neighbour to you? Do I do you any hurt? Doth my coming be any hindrance unto you? Why, then, do you vex me, by permitting and suffering your poor to cut down and carry away my wood out of my parks and grounds, and to sell the same?'

Mayor and magistrates excused themselves; poor people were so hard to keep in check. What could they do?

Do? They could whip the rogues, and punish those who had bought their lops and tops. ' Go,' his majesty growled; ' go, whip them all; not only those who steal, but those who buy. Hence! Whip them all!'

Thus mayor and vicar were dismissed; thus aldermen and country magistrates were turned against the court.

Year after year, men who rode their own geldings joined the marauders in the forest. Entering at night, with their hounds and servants, they singled out a stag and followed him, hushing their dogs, and deadening their horses' hoofs. Often these men were seen, and sometimes they were traced; but proofs were hard to find, and juries harder to convince. Two burghers, Richbell and Buckeridge, were indicted for killing deer in the royal forest. They were men of means, owning their own dogs and horses. Keepers and grooms gave evidence against them. There was hardly any doubt about their guilt, but their offence could not be proved in law. Richbell denied that he had coursed with greyhounds in the park by night. Buckeridge admitted that he might have killed some deer; but that was long ago; not less than six or seven years ago. A servant swore that he had buried a deer-skin for Buckeridge's man, but this evidence was turned by a neighbour, who swore he saw that deer killed, accidentally, by a dog. Nothing was gained by these attempts. Windsor was sore about her vicar, and the royal town turned more and more against the king: yet James went down to his grave unconscious of the tempest which his policy was raising around St. George's keep.

James sowed the wind; his son, and his son's sons, were to reap the storm.

CHAPTER XI.

BOOK OF SPORTS.

1633-5.

THIRTY years after the first Stuart came to Windsor, Charles put out his Book of Sports: 'The king's majesty's Declaration to his subjects concerning lawful sports to be used.' By lawful sports, the king and his advisers wished to be understood to mean Sunday sports.

In thirty years, the Stuarts, father and son, had wrought the most singular miracle ever seen on English ground:—for they had turned the hearts of thousands and tens of thousands away from the love of sport. Bowls, nine-pins, may-poles, archery, and races, were discarded things, which people of the 'better sort' were led to lay aside. The change was only for a time. We are a staid and vigorous race, with suckers running deep into the soil. If cut and staked, we grow again from the old root, and bring forth seed according to the stock. Clipping a branch will not transform a tree. Yet, for a season, Windsor, like other places, far and distant, underwent a change. Where was the jocund spirit that in merrie England used to laugh and lighten our greens and market-places from Dover to the Tweed? That jocund spirit was gone. Streets grew dull, and burgesses sour of face.. Light words were seldom heard. Laughter was divorced from life, and the domestic angels, humour and charity, were driven from the door. No longer blithe of heart, the housewives seemed to have forgotten their ancient creed:

'We may be merry and yet honest too.'

The younger race of matrons dressed in drab, cast down their eyes, and put on 'serious' looks. No frolic streamed along their veins. A dark and mournful genius seemed to stand beside them and to rule their lives. A Windsor wife, in the reign of Charles the First, could not have pardoned such a sinner as Sir John. In the collision of sects and parties, some of the finer charities were crushed.

Here, in the town books, lurk some glimpses of a Stuart Windsor, tenanted by another race to that of the merry men whom Shakespere knew and drew :

H. Asson and A. Triste, fined two shillings for playing nine-pins in service time.

R. Sea and four others, fined five and sixpence for playing catt in the park meadows at service time.

G. Strowd, fined one shilling for swearing.

W. Foster, fined one shilling for loitering in the park in service time.

J. Thorningby, fined two shillings for having persons tippling in his house.

Thorningby's wife and ten others, fined eleven shillings for not going to church.

In Queen Elizabeth's reign, such persons would have gone to church, because they were not driven. The church, instead of being in arms against the world, moved at her side, as her appointed work and walk. She taught and healed by her own graces, seeking no help from either mulct or whip. Under that open rule, Windsor was not only merrier, but more docile. Every one was with the law. A higher order reigned than that imposed by fines and stocks. Good men were of a common mind ; true to the church and loyal to the crown.

Under the Stuarts, Windsor was parting into sects and camps. Saints and sinners had long existed in the town ; the spirit of Testwood breathing on the saints ; the spirit of Simon resting on the sinners. Yet the sectaries were few in number and poor in strength, until the undue leaning of court towards papistry had driven a portion of the 'better sort' into the puritan lines. Marco had made a host of puritans. As they grew strong, they used their might in punishing offenders on the other side. Seated on the bench, severely staid, the sons of Page and Ford fined the successors of Nym and Pistol, when these loose companions, giving way to beer and tobacco, slunk into the Antelope yard for nine-pins, and strolled into the meadow for a turn at catt.

Between these saints and sinners, Charles and his advisers took up ground in the Book of Sports ; the most illogical act in an illogical career. Charles saw that men preferred play to prayer. He wanted them to pray. A penal statute drove them towards the church ; no penal statute drove them towards the tavern yard and village green. They took the broad way out of choice. It seemed to him a natural preference, springing from original sin and the depravities of the human heart. It was a sign of evil, but he thought the evil might be turned to good. Suppose he wedded prayer to play, and made the church an adjunct of the ale-house and village green?   Suppose he ordered Sunday games, but made the joining in these sports depend on a man's attendance at his parish church ?   Might not the Tristes, who loved nine-pins, and the Seas, who preferred catt, be lured to sermon by a promise of winding up the service with their favourite sport ?

A form lay close at hand.   Fifteen years ago, in the first days of Marco's residence at Windsor, James had drawn up a Book of Sports, with the design of introducing catholic manners.   Chiefly through the steadiness of Abbot, that scheme had failed, and after Marco's expulsion, had been dropped.   But Abbot was no more, and Laud was in his place.   Laud, a 'son' of Marco, was an ardent advocate of the list of sports.   The book was found, reprinted, and, with added paragraphs, launched into the world.   Few printed books have made so vast a stir.

No feudal monarch ever stretched authority more foolishly than Charles.   Pastimes were imposed.   No man was free to take his choice.   Games were allowed and disallowed.   Men and women were allowed to dance.   Men were allowed to shoot, to leap, to vault.   Neither men nor women were to bait bulls and bears.   May-games, Whitsun ales, and morris-dancers were allowed.

Everything was to be done by rule and order; everything at the appointed time and place. Charles was too frail in animal strength to feel the delight men have in doing what they like, and when they like. He never dreamed that men who could not be driven to church, might equally object to be driven to the village green.

The rule was carried out on feudal lines. Each village was to keep within itself; dancing on its own green, under the shade of its own church. A rustic from beyond the brook or hedge was not to join in the village sports. He ought to be at home, with his own people, under the eyes of his own minister, not gadding into distant parts. Who could be sure that he had been at church? Either straying from church or stealing after village lass, he was at fault, and must be driven away. Thus neighbourhood and courtship were destroyed, and village green set up in arms against village green.

Each parish was divided into portions : people of 'good' repute, and people of 'bad' repute. People of good repute were those who said yes to everything the parson said ; people of bad repute were those who disputed what the parson said. That parson might be high-church or low-church

—high as Goodman, or low as Martin—but if persons went to hear him preach they were of good repute, and had a right, under the Book of Sports, to dance on the village green.

The sectaries, whether puritan or papist, were excluded from the green. No prayer, no play. This rule was absolute. A man of good repute was not to dance and leap, to shoot and vault, unless he had been at church that day. Men were denounced as 'unworthy of any lawful recreation, that will not come to church.'

With some simplicity, James had stated what he thought these Sunday sports would do for him. They would turn men's hearts towards religion; they would train men's limbs for war; they would occupy men's leisure time; and they would stop men's tongues.

Charles, like his father, counted on the policy of silencing men's tongues. Dancers on village greens were likely to leave politics alone; while gossips at an ale-house porch were likely to use their wits on king and councillors. Among forbidden games stood bowling; not on Sunday only, but on every day alike. The 'meaner sort' were not to touch a bowl; the game being called a courtly game. The better reason was, that bowling-greens were being turned into conventicles. Yielding to the wishes of their customers, the owners were entertaining preachers in their houses, to expound the Scriptures in the interval of game and game. Bowling-greens were growing into theological and political clubs.

The king's book was ordered to be read from the pulpit of every parish church, and bishops and clergy were commanded to see it carried out. After divine service, every rector and incumbent was to lead his congregation out. Instead of closing the holy day with hymn and prayer, they were to rally at the butts and on the green, and end their day amidst the laughter of village damsels and the bawls of village swains. Men who were far from being sectaries, shuddered at the levities in the king's book.

Because the court was French, were parish priests to force French manners on their flocks?

Laud insisted on his rule. The book was ordered to be read and must be read. No plea of conscience moved him. What was ordered to be done, should not be left undone. Some bishops tried to smooth things over, and to bring in feudal habits of obedience step by step. The king, they taught, should be obeyed in things not openly against the word of God ; but hundreds of their parish clergy answered that the king's injunctions were against the word of God. Some refused compliance. Others allowed their clerks to read the order. Not a few complied, with a dramatic postscript to the royal text. Having read the words aloud, they closed the book, and said :

' That is the injunction of man.'

Then opening the service book, they read the fourth commandment, ' Remember thou keep holy the Sabbath day ; ' and closing it with reverence added :

' That is the word of God.'

Every county in England had a host of martyrs. Berkshire, like every other, was up in arms ; the women, as in all church matters, being fiercer than the men. Lambe, dean of the arches, was informed by one of his correspondents, that the women about Windsor banned and cursed him to the pit of·hell.

All papists in disguise—from Laud to Wren, from Wren to Goodman—were in favour of the book ; all puritans, avowed or secret, were against the book ; but neither party saw that it was doomed to fail.

Nobody went to church, in order that he might

afterwards have a romp. When told to play, people refused to play. Sport, when forced on them by kings and priests, became as hateful in their eyes as a constable's staff. They left it off, and made a game of giving up all games.

No other act of Charles made so many puritans as his Book of Sports.

CHAPTER XII.

WINDSOR CROSS.

1635 - 40.

OUTSIDE the Castle-gate, in High Street, stood a cross, which had been first erected in the times of Cardinal Beaufort—not by that son of John of Gaunt, or even by a monastic builder—but by plain John Sadler, mason and inhabitant of the town.

Chaucer had hailed that cross when it was fresh from the builder's hand; Shakespere had seen it wasted and crumbling to the ground. Built in a good period, the art was rich and rare; of kin to that which lighted up Cheapside. But wind and rain had done their work at Windsor as elsewhere, and Sadler's edifice was now a wreck. No one had cared to injure what remained. Old and harmless, free from paint and crucifix, the pile offended no man's conscience, and was suffered to sink into the earth in peace. But now, as many people thought, the olden times were coming back : the days of Cardinal Pole, if not of Cardinal Beaufort. Charles seemed bringing in the feudal monarchy. Laud appeared to be setting up the mediæval church. If king and primate had their way, the times of Cardinal Beaufort would return. The courtly priests were willing to go and meet those coming times half way ; times figured to the mental eye by Father Leonard and the Capuchin friars. No priest at Windsor was more eager to go out and meet them than Canon Goodman, pupil and representative ot the apostate dean. His method was an offer to rebuild the Windsor cross.

Goodman had an object to obtain.

Few men knew better than the canon what was passing in the King's house. Both Charles and Henrietta were attached to Windsor, which they made their nursery, their play-ground, and their school. At Windsor they were free from some of the suspicious eyes that rested on them at Whitehall. And they had much to hide from public sight. The queen was not a catholic only, but a chosen agent of her church—the Esther of her race, the Clothilde of her faith—blessed by the Pope for her appointed task—the rearing of a line of catholic kings. Charles had consented that his children should be taught by catholics till they were old enough to choose a creed! But though the king was base enough to give his word, he had not been bold enough to keep it. Vexed at his own weakness, he was trying to trick his wife, who charged him with his breach of faith, and tried to trick him in her turn, by placing 'concealed catholics' about his sons. To Mary, her daughter, she gave a rosary, with a hint to hide it carefully from every one except the Capuchins. Her boys and girls were trained to hide their thoughts. One of her women had the task of filling Mary with catholic sentiments, which she was told to do by dwelling on the two great facts, that her mother was a catholic, and that her husband would be a catholic. The child soon fell into her snares. 'Take me to mass, I shall be glad to go.' One day, an attendant hurried her to the queen's chapel, where Capuchins were saying mass. She knelt, and stayed the service out, as though she had done so all her days. The tale got wing and frightened Charles, who had begun to dream of the Prince of Orange for a son-in-law. No prince of that great house would take a girl who was attending mass. The women's pranks were stopped. But if the girl was lost, the queen felt certain of her sons. The boys were plain of face and loud of tongue. Charles, the elder born, was bursting with whim and mischief, while James, his younger brother, seemed a magazine of brooding and suspicious thoughts. 'Clothilde' was right; both were secured for Rome. Love of the world might tempt her elder son into evasion and concealment, but in secret he would hold on to her church, and when the moment came, would die in her embrace. In James, the younger lad, the system of evasion and concealment was to end.

Aware of all these doings in the royal house, Goodman proposed to meet the feudal times half way, by offers to rebuild the Windsor cross.

Apt pupil of his master, Marco, he had made a ruling principle of the moralities of a corsair port. All men, he held, are rogues, and if you want them you must pay their price. A bargain may be open or concealed—a bribe direct or roundabout—but you must always bring the money in your hand. Here is a picture of the man, drawn in a story by himself:

A part of the Castle wall behind the canon's lodgings fell into the dean's garden. As the tenements were unsafe, petitions were presented to the Crown, and orders issued to repair the waste. But months passed by, and nothing more was done. The dean wrote letters, and the canons teased their friends for help. All sorts of promises were made; yet neither carpenter nor mason fell to work. At every meeting of the chapter the affair was raised, till one of the canons (understood to be himself) rose in the chapter-house and said: 'The times are such that we churchmen are thought to be very simple, as compared with lawyers; and the reason is, that our wit is bounded by honesty, and that theirs is not.' The dean and canons must have held their breath while the enlightened priest went on to say what *he* would have them do: 'Men must now bribe, that they may have and enjoy their own. Instead of writing letters and making friends, I would buy a purse, put in it a hundred pieces, and present it to some great lord.'

By acting on this principle he had thriven in the church. From Marco he had got the Vicarage of West Ildsley; from James he had got the deanery of Rochester and the bishopric of Gloucester. By a proper use of money, he had been able to keep his vicarage of Ildsley and his canonry at Windsor, in addition to his see. It was a scandal, but the church authorities shut their eyes. So far, he had walked with Laud, and found protection in the friends of Laud. Yet, in his own opinion, his advance was slow. For ten years he had held a third-rate see. His eyes were fixed on London, Winchester, and Durham. How was he to win a higher grade? Once, he had been very near success. Seeing the king distressed by the wandering of his people from their parish church, he had done a stroke of business which had won the heart of Charles.

Under the window of his lodging lay that meadow in which Testwood had been burnt. To this spot came the travelling preachers, who denounced the Book of Sports. Men who had sat under Martin, listening to his sober words, were straying to the meadow, where they heard Love-the-Lord Smith, and Help-on-High Fox, call fire of heaven on all the evil-doers in high places, who profaned the Sabbath day. Charles met the evil by doing what his father had refused to do; making a small provision for the minister of their church. A fellowship was found for Martin; not at Windsor, where Dean Wren, a catholic in everything but name, refused to have him—but at Eton College, where the liberal Wotton held the provost's chair. The king's grace came too late. Even at Eton the vice-provost and a batch of Fellows raised a cry against receiving Martin, though the vicar was a dying man. Eton was disturbed, but Windsor was not pacified.

Here lay the canon's hope. Few of these wanderers from the parish church were fanatics; they were simply men and women over whom the Church was losing her former grip. Not having wandered far, they might be called into the fold once more; though not by fines and Sunday sports. The serious mind must be allured by serious things. Suppose he gave an organ to their church? St. George's Chapel had a noble organ; but the mayor and burgesses—'Townhead, Clod, and Puppy'—came no longer to St. George's Chapel. Goodman thought an organ, finely played, would lure them back. And he was right. The king was greatly pleased, and in his gladness offered him the see of Hereford. But Marco's spirit reigned so strongly in his convert, that he gave offence, and lost the whole of his expected gain, by asking for a license to hold both sees—at least, for a single year.

Two bishoprics in one hand! This was, indeed, going back to the times of Cardinal Pole. For one who was already rector of West Ildsley, canon of Windsor, and bishop of Gloucester, to add a second bishopric to his pluralities, was too much. Charles withdrew his offer, drove the canon out of Windsor, and admonished him to live in future on his diocese.

That over-greed had been his great mistake in life. Was he to find a second chance? Yes; in the Windsor cross.

Outside his palace-gate, a cross was rising from the ground. It was a pretty and artistic thing. Why not do something similar at Windsor? Charles was fond of art. The old town cross was dropping into dust; suppose he offered to rebuild that cross? Already he had gained a footing with the burgesses. Jones, the mayor, had no opinions of his own. Windsor was the royal residence; a cross outside the Castle-gate would be often under Charles's eye. It was a catholic sign, and everything in the Castle proved that catholic rites were coming in. 'Clothilde' had her chapel and her Capuchins; mass, vespers, complines, were said at Windsor much as they were said in Paris. Most of the ladies near the queen were catholics, and these ladies had the nursing of future kings. Goodman believed that nothing save fear prevented

Charles from joining the communion of his wife. The canon's course was therefore clear.

Jones, and 'the better sort,' had no objection to receive his gift. Crosses are older than the papacy. Our Saxon fathers were familiar with the Runic cross. Cortez found the cross in Mexico; and Indian crosses were erected long before the birth of Christ. In England, roods or crosses had been used as marks; set up at forking roads, in market-places, and at city gates. Nothing in either history or legend set men's hearts against a cross. So Goodman's offer was applauded, and his masons fell to work. But, as his pile grew up, men noticed that his masons were erecting in their High Street an edifice utterly unlike John Sadler's work. A crucifix started up, where no such thing had been before. Two sides of the pile were covered by paintings; one picture, that of a crucifixion, another, that of a resurrection. Over these paintings ran a scroll in gilt letters :

'JESUS NAZARENUS REX JUDÆORUM.'

Here was flat popery! A meeting of 'the better sort' took place. Some burgesses declared that such things were against the law, and that the mayor might have to answer for them in a public court. By resolution, Jones was required to tell his lordship, in the name of the whole town, that he must either stop his masons, or produce a license from the king. Goodman replied with scorn. They had his plans, he said, and everything had been done with their consent. Let them take care. Once, at least, they had been rebuked for leaning towards the Puritans. They had better not offend again. As for the law, he took that burden on himself. After his scolding, he returned to his more worldly vein. See what they were doing— turning good money from their town! He meant to spend five times as much. See how they were dealing with the poor, whom he intended to employ and pay!

His threats and bribes were all too late. The burgesses denounced him to the king, and asked that his pictures should be smeared, his crucifix taken down. In hopes of staying this evil, he returned to Windsor, and resumed his lodgings in the lower ward. At once the town sprang up, and a petition to expel him from his house was laid before the king. Charles felt annoyed. Instead of doing good the Windsor cross had done him harm. The town seemed turned into one huge conventicle. A scapegoat being needed, Goodman was expelled a second time. Windsor saw his face no more ; though of his name and cross they were to hear again.

CHAPTER XIII.

IN THE FOREST.

1641.

' Insolences in the Forest' were reported to the king; insolences which were always brisk, and sometimes jovial; sounds of an approaching conflict, caught more readily by the Constable on the keep than by the courtiers in the King's house.

Aminadab Harrison and Thomas Patey, men who assumed the parts of Robin Hood and Little John, were leading him a dance of sport and mischief.

Never, since the night when James had closed his Little park, and turned the people of his neighbourhood into critics and enemies, had the Forest known one hour of peace. The Constable locked his gates; the squires and better sort made private keys, and entered like the ' gentlemen of the highest quality.' He changed his locks, on which they broke his fences with as little scruple as the tramps. The game and wood became prize of war. A bold man snapped his prey—stag, rabbit, lop and top—and carried what he seized away. Scores of raiders followed Richbell and Buckeridge; breaking into the chase with horse and hound, less because they cared for venison than because they delighted in lawless sport. Men who dropt dancing on village greens, as soon as dancing was 'allowed,' had no objection to marauding in the king's forest on Sunday night. Filching wood went on; trapping game went on. By day, the Forest was the king's; by night, the king's authority disappeared. His stakes were carried off and burnt. In vain his woodmen set them up; work done by day was overthrown by night. His pale being down, the grass lay open to all comers. Cattle strayed into the pastures; vagabonds brought in their donkeys; farmers let their horses stray. An unfenced ground is soon considered ' waste; ' a sort of no-man's land, on which the houseless wanderer had a right to squat. In olden time, before the forest was enclosed, no vagrant dared to burrow in the earth, or roost under a pile of wood. Every man's dog was then a hunter of such game, every man's gun a peril

to such lodgers. When the glades grew into
solitudes, in which foxes and badgers found their
lairs, vagrants, hardly less savage than foxes and
badgers, sought in them a home. Four squatters,
male and female, of the name of Milton, got a foot-
hold in the forest, and refused to be expelled.
Grubbing under the roots of trees, they stood at
bay, with pike and gun. No verderer liked to
tackle them, for blood was certain to be shed.
Like shepherds in King Edward's time, they ate
the king's game, and made a joke of squatting on
his land. Living as outlaws, paying no rent, and
taking what they called their own, they set the
verderers and keepers at defiance. No man liked
to risk his life; and public feeling ran so high
against the system, that the keepers feared to execute their trust. A keeper, who had done his
duty, was in trouble. Finding a rustic in the act
of stealing wood, he flew at him, beat him soundly,
and drove him from the park. The rustic died;
the town took up his case. A sergeant was
despatched to bring the keeper in; the man resisted, and the sergeant was repulsed. Advised by
sympathisers in the town, he brought an action for
assault. The keeper pleaded in defence that he
believed the man to be a poacher and wood-stealer;

but the jury found him guilty, and the magistrates fined him seven pounds, with imprisonment till the fine was paid. The Castle tried to take him from the town. He was a prisoner in another court, to which the town must give him up, said the Castle; but the town refused, and kept the prisoner in their jail.

No man was more impressed by these ' insolences in the forest ' than the Constable, who heard the mutterings of a tempest from his platform on the Norman keep.

Rich, earl of Holland, Constable of Windsor, stood in the highest favour with king and queen. A younger son of Lady Rich—one of the two boys which her complaisant spouse had been pleased to own—he was born alike to penury and to favour. Patting his pretty check, James had filled his pockets from the public chest, married him to a great heiress, and ennobled him as baron Kensington and earl of Holland. Gazing in rapture on his fine form, Charles had made him Groom of the Stole, Knight of St. George, Constable of Windsor, and Lord Justice in Eyre. Seldom in the roll of favourites had Groom and Constable been more perfect creations of the royal will. To Henrietta, he was no less dear than to Charles. Holland had courted her for the king ; and scandal added, for himself. Her majesty showed as keen an eye for beauty in the other sex as her great father, Henri Quatre. Holland was allowed to be the handsomest man at court. She made him steward of her lands and manager of her revenues ; places of trust which drew him to her cabinet for daily talk. Keen eyes observed that Holland had more of her private leisure than she gave to either Jermyn or Digby.

As Lord Justice in Eyre, this man was chief ranger, not of the Forest only, but of every park and chase below the Trent. All that was done under the forest laws was done by him. He staked the grounds—stocked them with deer—and drove the rustics out by force. Men who were whipt and mulcted laid their injuries at his door. If a new district was imparked, his shoulders had to bear the blame. To say he was unpopular is nothing. He was followed by such curses as pursued the path of Laud.

A sensitive and timid man, he listened with nervous terror to the rising gale, uncertain of his safety, even behind the guns and battlements of the Norman keep. Castle or country—which, he asked himself, was going to be the stronger side?

The Constable was not the only man who put that question to himself. Here, in the town books, stand brief entries—not without a touch of humour :

'Given the ringers on the king's birthday, three shillings.

'Paid for two books for the Fast at the beginning of parliament, one shilling and eight pence.

'Given the ringers on the king's coronation day, three shillings.

'Paid for a prayer for good success of the parliament, four pence.'

Holland was unaided by the local magistrates. Aminadab was Robin Hood; his men were assertors of public law. Severe against catt and nine-pins, mayor and aldermen were lenient when they had to deal with intruders in the royal chase.

Windsor, as Holland knew, was like all other places standing at the gates of royal parks. Round every chase in the southern counties feuds had broken out, and rustic battles had been fought. Bad blood had everywhere sprung up, and men were learning to regard the sovereign chiefly in connexion with his forest-laws. As years rolled on, the bitter feeling had extended from the king to his lieutenants—to the peers and gentry, sheriffs and magistrates. In every county, parks were attacked,

deer killed, woods burnt, walls levelled to the grass.
Rioters were hung by tens and dozens ; yet the
course of outrage never stopped. A man was hung :
a band sprang up to carry on his work. Women
found in the parks were clapped in jail ; on which
their kinsfolk burned the sheriff's barn. Gibbets
were built at every cross-road, yet gangs of men,
strong enough to defy village constables, roamed
about the country breaking down enclosures and
firing hay-ricks. Where the deer were scanty, they
fed on flocks of sheep. May-poles gave place to
hanging-trees ; yet year by year the Robin Hoods
and Little Johns increased in strength.

Holland got scared. So long as things were
calm at Windsor no man was so gay as he. Riots
in the midland counties were now no more to him
than disturbances in Hungary or in Spain ; but
Windsor Forest lay within his ken ; Aminadab's
doings startled him in the night. He told his story
to his peers. The trespassers, he said, had stolen
more than a hundred deer ! What was he to do ?

' Disperse them,' said the lords ; ' if they refuse,
arrest them in the act and bring them up to town.'

The Constable thought his majesty was entering
on ' a dangerous course.'

CHAPTER XIV.

WINDSOR SEIZED.

1642.

Wednesday:

Wednesday, January twelfth, the date on which his majesty 'seized' Windsor Castle, was the opening day of the Civil War.

On Monday afternoon, six days after his failure to arrest Lord Mandeville and the Five Members, he had left Whitehall, and taking coach, had snapped up his son, the prince, and driven by way of Hampton Court to Windsor, which he reached on Wednesday afternoon at dusk. The days were dark, the roads were rough. His journey in the depth of winter had the aspect of a flight, almost of a rout.

Beside him were the queen, the two princes, Charles and James, the princess Mary, and a few officers and domestics; headed and followed by a troop of 'cavaliers.' No royal train brought up the rear, with lords and ladies two or three hundred coaches long ; only that troop of horse, with Colonel Lunsford, the Sussex giant, in their front. These horsemen were a motley group ; free-lances, picked up here and there by Digby ; some in city taverns, others in foreign camps ; bold riders and hard hitters all of them ; soldiers well fitted by their broken fortunes for a desperate enterprise. Luns-ford was worthy of his troop. Big, ugly, one-eyed, he had been nicknamed the Devourer of Children. Lately appointed by the king Lieutenant of the Tower, he had been dismissed from his important post, on the petition of Lords and Commons, as a man of infamous character. He was burning for revenge.

No man saluted Charles ; no damsel curtsied to the queen. Driving through the streets, their majesties passed the gates in silence. Windsor, outside these castle walls, seemed lost.

They were prepared for this defection of the town ; but not for a defection in the royal house. No Constable stood beside the gate to bid them welcome, and to go before them to the upper ward. Holland hung back ; that creature of the king's bounty being the first to fall away. Charles, on setting out, had sent for him to attend his person and discharge the duties of his place. He made excuses ; pleading his engagements in the House of Lords. It was a bitter day for Charles ; the first of many bitter days to come.

Closing the gate, and posting sentries on the wall, he went up into the gallery, where, if shorn of regal pomp, he felt secure against a rush of pikes. No Venn could scale the Tudor tower ; no Skippon force the Norman keep. Here in his feudal stronghold, he was still a feudal king.

The queen, enraged against peers and commoners for having closed her chapel and lodged her confessor, Philip, in the Tower, was hot for strife. Esthers and Clothildes are never timid, and not often cool. 'It is my war, my sacred war,' she said of the impending fray. She had implored her husband to arrest the members :—' Pull me those rascals out by the ears.'   When Charles came back to her baffled, with the tears of failure in his eyes, she had urged him to send for Digby, and to act on his advice. Digby was her officer, as Strafford had been his officer. Charles disliked the man, but, yielding to her passion, he had suffered him to be called.

Digby's theories were feudal and heroic ; worthy

of the time of Hawkwood and the brain of Huntingdon. 'Withdraw the guard; secure the prince; seize Windsor castle, and your majesty may command your kingdom,' was his brief and bold advice. If Charles would suffer him to act, he swore that he would raise an army, crush the City companies, and pitch the Lords and Commons into the Thames.

His army was to resemble the old Free Companies, the old brigades of St. George. His majesty was to run no risk; to give no pledge, to sign no paper, that could be brought against him. Digby took the peril on himself. The service was to be his own; the profits were to be the king's. He staked his head on his success.

So he had sworn; and so the king had done; not trusting him, yet giving him a chance in order to appease the queen.

Windsor was gained, and yet the roads outside appeared to Charles as cheery as the rooms within. Vainly his eye ran up and down; cabinet, presence-chamber, gallery, were all deserted by the customary groups. Where were his bishops, councillors, and officers of state? Some were in exile; some in prison; not a few were sitting with his enemies. Others, hardly less dear to him than his Constable, had fallen off. Hertford was in Westminster; Essex was in Westminster.

The king had wounded Hertford by his way of snatching up the prince. A kinsman of the royal house, Hertford bad been appointed governor to the Prince of Wales, as being a man of large experience and exalted rank. He was responsible for the prince's person; yet the king, coming on him suddenly, had snatched his charge away. 'If they have our son, they will have all,' the queen had cried, when Charles appeared to falter. Hertford was too prudent for 'heroic' measures. He had suffered exile and imprisonment. Though loyal to his king, he was not a man to risk his liberty and life in anybody's cause except his own. The king had yielded to his wife and carried off his son; leaving his servant to fume and fret; to sit with other peers, who, neither papists like South-ampton, nor puritans like Mandeville, were voting every day more steadily against the king and queen.

No less wide a gap was caused by the non-appearance of Essex. This eminent soldier held the chamberlain's staff. Like Holland, he had been called to attend the king; like Holland, he had disobeyed his majesty's command. These peers were first cousins; Essex a nephew, Holland a son, of Lady Rich ; but in their walks of life they had seldom journeyed by a common road. Essex was a soured and wretched man, cursed by a second wife as false to him as the first. A woman-hater, he despised society, and passed his time in studying war and in the exercise of arms. His cousin was a thing of courts and courtly companies ; yet for once the sombre captain and the sprightly courtier were united in a single thought. Each held aloof from Digby's enterprise.

Though hurt by both, the king was far less sore against his lord chamberlain than against his constable of Windsor. Essex was an independent peer. Service, and not preference, had given him the staff. In truth, the king had treated him with levity ; one day sending him into the field as his lieutenant, next day dismissing him with a bluntness bordering on contempt. Yet Essex bore no malice in his breast. So long as he could serve the crown without betraying his country, he retained his office. When forced to choose between the crown and country, he resigned. The king admitted that his course was eminently fair. Refusing to join the king at Windsor, he returned his staff. The letter was in Charles' hand — the signature hardly dry.

The queen advised her husband to accept his offer, and appoint another chamberlain in his place. For Holland she could find excuses, but for Essex she saw none. Charles paused and weighed the matter well; for he was on the verge of war, and Essex, who had served in the Palatinate, had a great repute in arms. Could he afford to break with the first captain in his realm?

Digby, according to his plan, had drawn a portion of the guards from Westminster to Kingston, and secured the bridge. 'King's friends' were rallying on that point; men who rode their own geldings, carried their own arms, and brought their own grooms into the field. They had already occupied the taverns and broken open the magazines. Lunsford, the one-eyed colonel, was to be their chief; but, in his absence with the king's party, Howard was acting in his name. A camp was to be formed in rear of Windsor, on the plain of Aldershot. Two hundred captains and colonels were reported to be waiting for their companies and regiments. At a word from Windsor, all these companies and regiments were expected to start up. So Digby swore, and so the queen believed. Clothildes are apt to be strong in faith.

But Charles was not prepared to speak that

word.   A word from Windsor might do much ; but such a word meant war—not in another name, to be disavowed in case of failure, but his own. If blood was shed by his command, the battle must be fought at once, and he must stake his crown and life, as other kings had staked their crowns and lives.   The day for such a trial might arrive, and he was bound to look beyond the day.   All other means might fail.

His wisdom was to keep his captain in reserve. Essex at Windsor would be worth five thousand men.   The more his majesty thought, the more he saw good reason to reject the queen's advice. What could he gain by calling in a courtly favourite ?   So long as Essex held the staff— though it were but in name—there was a chance of drawing him to Windsor. By refusing to accept the resignation, he would have the appearance of regarding Essex as a faithful servant.   Such an appearance might create suspicion in the House of Lords ; and Digby might have no more dangerous enemy to meet than Venn or Skippon.   In the hope of drawing Essex to his side, he laid that letter of resignation in his desk.

Sitting at that moment with their peers, his Chamberlain and Constable were engaged in passing orders that no guns, no stores, no powder, no provisions should be moved from any of the royal magazines, except on the 'king's warrant — signed by the two Houses of Parliament ;' a form of grim political humour hardly to be matched in any comedy on the Windsor stage.

When his majesty was housed, his followers took possession of the town ; his captains marching on the Garter and the White Hart; his men invading the Antelope, Crown, and other taverns ; where they drank the king's health, and roared perdition to the crop-ears, through the winter night. For them the sword was drawn ; the Civil War begun.

CHAPTER XV.

UNDER THE KEEP.

1642.

Thursday:

Waking under cover of the Norman keep, the king felt safer in his person than he had done for many days; yet his Intelligence from Westminster showed him how closely he was watched, and how well his moves were known.

On both sides the Intelligence was minute and rapid; more so on the popular side than on the royalist side. Every ante-room at Windsor fed a spy. In Lady Suffolk's time, every page and abigail had learnt the price of news, and how to turn a screen, a key-hole, or an alley, into current coin. A secret known to three persons was regarded by a prudent councillor as unsafe. Never in England had corruption soared so high, and sunk so low, as under James and Charles. Love, greed, religion, everything seemed to feed this leprosy. Startled by the speed with which his private words were sold, the king exclaimed: 'Neither at my table, nor about my garden, nor in my cabinet, can I trust myself to speak.' Lady Carlisle, the nearest person to her majesty, had betrayed his design of seizing the Five Members; and Holland, the nearest person to himself, had carried her message to his enemies. His only comfort was, that those who sold his secrets, brought him back news, which he considered of the utmost moment, from the other side.

From his Intelligence he learnt that, while he was driving yesterday on his road to Windsor, a man named Calcott had been giving the House of Commons an account of his affairs at Kingston; naming Digby, Lunsford, and Howard, as his chief officers; describing the condition of his men, the stabling of his horses, and the movements of his powder-carts. Motions, he learned, had followed on the heels of this report. Digby had been denounced to his peers. Lunsford had been voted a Malignant, and an officer deputed to bring him in. Howard, a member of the House, had been ordered to attend, and answer at the bar. Events were coming on him with a rush, and there was little time for Digby to prepare his plans.

Later in the day, as the Intelligence showed, a man named Lee, employed on the Thames, gave notice to the Commons, that several barges, laden with war-saddles, were going up the stream towards Kingston bridge. Action no less prompt had followed Lee's report. A sergeant, taking two city companies in boats, was ordered to give chase, to seize those saddles, and prevent the passage up and down the river of suspicious craft.

The worst was yet to come. Four counties, Berks, Bucks, Middlesex, and Surrey, had been ordered out; the sheriffs being instructed to suppress the rioters at Kingston bridge, and to disperse all other assemblies of armed men within the shires. Digby's intention seemed to have been revealed, and force was evidently to be met by force.

Here came the test. What answer would the peers, the city companies, and the county bands, return to such audacious votes? Since Richmond's landing, no appeal of such importance had been made against a reigning prince. Surely those votes of peers and commoners would not be heard. He was their king; their crowned, anointed king. He was the master of all sheriffs and all musters. In the face of his 'divine' right, what man would dare to lift a pike against him? To oppose the Lord's anointed, was not only crime, but sin. His head was sacred; yet, in spite of his ' divinity,' he was hedged about with many fears.

Kingston lay in Surrey, and the bridge connected her with Middlesex. These shires might be concerned in looking after Lunsford's bands; but why were Bucks and Berks called out? Were they to march against his followers in the town?

Bucks and Berks were Windsor shires, lying around the King's house, much of them visible from St. George's keep. Not forty years ago, they were the loyallest section of the kingdom; every owner of a freehold sworn ' to live and die ' with Queen Elizabeth. Yet the Lords and Commons seemed to trust the king's own sheriffs, his own militia, living under his own ramparts, with the task of breaking up his volunteers by force!

His followers in the town, though swollen to five or six hundred men, were hardly better than a mob. Undrilled and poorly armed, they were unlikely to resist a charge. Suppose the men of Berks and Bucks obeyed that vote? His government, nay, his personal freedom, might be limited to the circuit of his Castle wall. Would they obey that vote?

An incident arose. Ten or twelve riders crossed the bridge, coming out of Bucks, and, working through the crowd in Thames Street, wheeled on their left, and halted at the Castle gates. An officer appeared. What did they want? To see the king. On what account? The business of their county. Who were they? Men of Bucks, deputed by the freeholders of Bucks.

Their presence was announced to Charles. He knew the men, and what they came about. Two days ago, as he had read in his Intelligence, they had cantered into Westminster, four thousand strong; well drilled, well armed, and resolute men, with tenders of their service as a body-guard to the peers and commoners. Thanked for a service which the peers and commoners no longer needed, they had asked that all bishops and all papist lords should be expelled from parliament. Being told that these demands should be considered, they had further said, they had a petition to present, and hoped the House would either send it to the king, or tell them where to carry it. Lenthall, the Speaker, glad to be rid of his visitors, had begged them to ride home, select ten or twelve deputies, and send them into Windsor with a humble request to see his majesty.

These deputies of Bucks were at his gate. Had he felt strong enough, he would have scattered them with shot. Only two days since, they had taken oaths ' to live and die ' with his opponents. To disperse them with a volley would have given him great delight; but they were backed by thousands of their neighbours; and a crash of musketry from the towers and walls in Thames Street might bring in the armed militia of two counties. Though he loathed the rascals, he must smooth his brow and speak them fair. Digby would have hurled them from the Castle wall; but Charles adopted a milder and a wiser course.

Falling into one of those pensive moods and picturesque attitudes which his artists liked to paint, he sent an usher to conduct the deputies to his cabinet. The men were grave and rustic; not to be overcome by pensive smiles and picturesque clothes. What they had come to say, they said. Under his majesty's writ, their spokesman told him, they had chosen John Hampden for their knight of the shire. A man noted for his loyalty, he enjoyed their utmost confidence. To their amazement, they had lately heard that Hampden had been accused of treason, he, and four other

members of the lower House. On much consideration, they had found the method of impeachment
so illegal, that they had come to the conclusion
that so foul an accusation had arisen, not from any
fault of the five gentlemen, but from the spite of
men who disliked their zeal in serving the king and
state. That charge of treason they regarded as
levelled against themselves, no less than against
their knight. Therefore, they prayed his majesty
that John Hampden, and the other members, might
' enjoy the just privilege of parliament.'

Listening with gracious smile, his majesty tried
to turn their anger from himself. Just privilege !
Why, that was his own thought. So far was he
from touching ' privilege of parliament,' there was
nothing in the realm he had a greater wish to
strengthen and sustain. Where the law seemed
dubious, he was ready to waive his kingly right.
Even in the case now pending, he assured them he
had given up his proceedings for the sake of peace.
He wanted what was just, but only for the good
of all. No sooner had he heard a doubt expressed
about the law, than he commanded his Lord Keeper,
Lyttleton, to adopt some other course. The five
offending members would be shortly tried; and

then all men would see which side was in the right. His visitors, he said, would find his evidence so strong, that they would say he had no option but to prosecute. Yet, in his heart, he hoped the gentlemen would be able to prove their innocence. He felt no rancour towards them. As a prince, he had to guard the public weal; but when that interest was secured, his task was done.

On one point more, he wished them to be satisfied. Whether the gentlemen were guilty or not guilty, was their own affair. If they had fallen into treason, they must take the consequence; but their offences tainted no one else. His 'good subjects,' the men of Bucks, were not accountable for Hampden's crimes. Let him prove guilty or not guilty, his majesty's visitors were free from blame.

The men of Bucks retired: a little mollified, yet on their guard. When they recrossed the bridge, they found the county gathering under arms, with orders to disperse all bodies of men in arms—such groups as they had left in Thames Street, under the Castle wall.

Digby and Lunsford started for their posts. To gain some days, a messenger was sent by

Charles to Westminster, with honeyed and un-meaning phrases, such as he had spoken to the men of Bucks. So far, he could help his friends, without his hand being seen, his crown being risked.

CHAPTER XVI.

AT BAY.

1642.

Friday :

In Digby's plan of campaign, Windsor was to be head-quarters, with a strong fore-post at Kingston, holding the bridge and covering the first passage of the river above Westminster, while the main array was mustering in the rear at Aldershot, supported and supplied from Portsmouth. Goring, governor of Portsmouth, was supposed to have been overcome by the queen's blandishments. He was supposed to have undertaken either to throw open his gates to the king's forces, or to furnish them with stores and guns. King and prince were to reside at Windsor, as a safe asylum. Kingston lay within nine or ten miles of the Vauxhall magazines. An army in possession of Kingston bridge not only covered Windsor, but was free to march on the capital by either bank.

The first thing was to make head-quarters. If king and prince were not secure, nothing was secure.

How was the Castle to be rendered safe? Old gates, decaying walls, and empty magazines, were hardly elements of strength. Unlike Dover and the Tower, Windsor had ceased to be a place of arms, governed by a military code. Sometimes she had no Constable. Under the Stuarts, her Constables had been courtiers, and not soldiers. Buckingham had been Constable; Holland was now Constable. Windsor was a country house; noble and capacious, but unequal to a siege. Guns, powder, match and small-arms, were wanting. Stores, weapons, and provisions, must be drawn from other magazines—chiefly from the Ordnance office in the Tower.

Newport, Master of the Ordnance, was a younger son of Lady Rich; one of the three or four lads whom her uncertain husband had refused to own. Laughing in his face, she had confessed her guilt by giving the brat her lover's name, Montjoy. Like all her sons, the lad was born to favour. Merit he had none. Yet for his mother's sake, the fribble had been made an Irish baron and an English earl. He and his royal master had been boys together, and the king had trusted him as he had done his brother—the first deserter from his post. Was he a faithful man ?

Two of his brothers, Warwick and Holland, were in London, voting with the king's enemies. Warwick was a roystering sailor, who made his home on shore in play-houses and taverns, where he enjoyed the reputation of a saucy tongue, a heated temper, and a ready fist. Holland, on the contrary, was a lady's man, dainty in speech, pretty in face, and mincing in gait. Yet these two men, unlike in nature and in bearing, had been lured into a common camp. Was Newport like the elder sons of Lady Rich ?

' The earl of Newport,' was announced.

On quitting Whitehall for Windsor, Charles had given his Master of the Ordnance full instructions. Newport was to see Byron, his new Lieutenant of the Tower, and to secure his service and connivance in sending out supplies. Saddles were to be sent to Kingston ; powder and match to Windsor and Aldershot. Had he obeyed ?

Fluttering into the cabinet, he said he had come on that affair. He had been trying to do his best. With Byron's help, he had filled some barges on the river, and some waggons on the road. But he had been betrayed. The enemy had spies in every house. Digby was suspected, and his lodging had been searched. No one was safe. Byron had been summoned to attend the Houses, and on pleading the king's order not to leave his post, he had been sentenced for contempt. Skippon, with the city forces, had been ordered to invest the Tower. Boats were on the river; companies in Thames, Street and St. Catharine's fields. Byron was all but lost. What must be done? That was what he wished to know.

What had been done by Newport's peers?

A little, but not much. Southampton had raised a storm, but he had only made the mischief worse. ' Parliament,' he had said, in the debate on Byron's matter, ' have neglected their duty to the king, in the safety of his person ; ' but the other lords had made him eat his words. A resolution had been carried that ' this parliament have performed their duties to the king for the safety of his person.' It was only by his sitting in his place and voting with the rest, that Newport had himself escaped. But he was not quite free. Orders had been laid on him, at his peril, not to remove one sack of biscuit or one pad of powder from the magazines, without a royal warrant signed by both

Houses of parliament. They had given him leave to come to Windsor, but they had not given him leave to stay. Some papers in his office needed signatures, and they had given him leave to come and get them signed; but he was under orders to return that day. Would his majesty be pleased to sign the documents?

'Leave them with me,' sighed the king, and Newport bowed and sidled from the room.

Saturday :

Hertford rode into Windsor with a message from the Lords. His errand was unpleasant; but he had no choice in the affair. He was enjoined to separate the king and prince.

To tear the child from his father's sight ? He was commanded to resume his post ; to take the legal custody of his charge ; and to prevent his highness being carried to a foreign port. Peers and commoners were suspicious, and had put him to his task on peril of a breach of trust :—a trust that he would have to answer with his head.

Hertford was a cold and selfish man, whose conduct to his wife, Arabella Stuart, had covered him with public shame. For years he had been exiled, but at length he had been pardoned, suffered to come home, and welcomed by the court. Seeing how the king inclined, he had struck in smartly for prerogative. A marquisate was his reward; but he had yet another round to win; the coronet of his ancestor, the People's Friend. To gain his cap and sword, Hertford was ready to become the king's friend and the people's friend by turns. While Parliament was stronger than the Crown, he must obey that stronger power. When royalty looked up, the world would find him in his proper place.

He brought two orders from his peers:

1. 'That the Lord Marquis Hertford, appointed by his majesty governor of the prince, as he will answer the breach of that trust, that doth so immediately concern the present and future peace and safety of the three kingdoms, shall forthwith repair to the prince, and, according to the duty of his place, take care of him, and give his personal attendance on his highness, and shall be very watchful that he be not carried out of the kingdom.'

2. 'That the Marquis of Hertford shall attend the prince's highness to-morrow morning, according to this aforesaid order, and acquaint his majesty therewith, from both Houses of Parliament.'

The draught was bitter, and the queen refused

her portion of the cup. Resign her son—whom she had promised to make a catholic king—to be the prey of gospellers and puritans ! Was that to be the Esther of her race, the Clothilde of her church ? Nay ; she would rather lose her crown : —by which she meant her husband's crown. The king controlled his temper. He was not a burning zealot, and the peer was standing on his legal right. If Digby won, these moths of fortune should discover what it was to irritate a king.

Sunday :

Little had been done towards making Windsor safe. No guns, and not much powder, had been got. Some stragglers dropped into the town in search of drink and pay ; but not many of these stragglers brought in horse and arms. Most of them were in rags; old tramps and scarecrows, passing as soldiers who had served in Ulster and on the Rhine. To take them into pay, and drill them into companies, would be money and labour thrown away. Before they could be armed and trained for service, the occasion might have passed. In thirty days, Digby's Free Companies would be either master of London or scattered to the winds.

Monday :

Bad news came in. A trail of fugitives crossed the bridge and rolled up Thames Street; crowding the tavern yards, and filling the market-place with tumult. They reported that the bands at Kingston bridge were breaking up. Lunsford had been taken by the sergeant who was ordered to arrest him. He had made no fight. The sergeant had a warrant; Lunsford had no warrant. Law was with the sergeant, and the giant was deserted by his men. Even hireling troops expected to be cowed by a lawful flag. His fall was evidence the age of the Free Companies was passed.

The fugitives embarrassed Charles. They were his partisans, suffering for his sake; but to receive and help them would expose him to suspicion as a partner in their plots. To save himself, he must stand aloof, severely calm; free in his words and in his acts; ready to ' disavow ' his friends—if they should fail. His news from Westminster was no better than his news from Kingston. Byron had been brought before the House of Lords, and forced to answer on his knees. Lyttleton, the lord keeper, had asked him why he had refused to come the previous day. Kneeling at the bar, he had read a letter from the king, forbidding him to quit his post. That plea had been rejected. Newport, as the king had wished him, offered bail, but Byron had been sentenced and condemned. Charles was no longer master of the Tower.

Lunsford, his one-eyed monster, was in London, lying under guard.

Tuesday :

Digby's experiment of fighting with Free Companies had failed. On leaving Windsor, he had gone to Kingston and harangued his troops. The king, he told them, had withdrawn his forces from the capital, ' to prevent them being trampled in the dirt.' He thanked them, in his majesty's name, for rallying in his cause, and led them to imagine they were mustered into service under the protection of his flag. They had been painfully undeceived. Instead of being joined by the country bands, they saw the militia gathering round them from all quarters. They became impatient with their officers. No king appeared; no royal flag was raised ; no proclamation issued. Companies broke up, and scattered to their homes. Some stragglers took the roads for Windsor; others, the roads for Aldershot and Portsmouth. Digby had moved into the west, where he appealed for help to Goring ;

but that wily trickster was not going to lose his head for a woman's smile.　He pointed to the Hants and Sussex musters.　How was he to stand against two counties?　Digby was proclaimed a rebel to the king and state.

Rejected and repulsed on every side, the companies diminished and disappeared.

An expert in the saddle and familiar with the roads, Digby contrived to slip through the sheriff's hands, to reach the sea-shore, and to cross the sea in one of the royal whelps.

CHAPTER XVII.

FEUDAL CHURCH.

1642.

Monday, January 17th:

The feudal army was dissolved. Where was the feudal church?

Outside the Castle gates, in High Street, lay a heap of stones; wreckage of that cross which Goodman had set up—partly in atonement for his sin, partly as a pointer on the way towards Rome. Cross and crucifix had been overturned by the indignant burgesses, bent on blocking up the road against returning Cardinal Poles. That ruin was an emblem of the feudal church.

On Tuesday, news arrived at Windsor of a singular scene. The previous day, John Williams, archbishop of York, was brought to the bar, required to kneel before his peers as a delinquent; and on being allowed to rise, was asked to plead, guilty or not guilty, to a charge of high treason. After pleading not guilty, he was put aside, while Goodman, bishop of Gloucester, Wren, bishop of Ely, and nine other prelates, were brought in one by one, compelled to kneel, and answer to a similar charge. On pleading not guilty, they besought the lords to grant them a speedy trial and to let them out on bail. A day was named for trial, but their bail was stubbornly refused. The night was cold, and many of the bishops were in feeble health. No courtesy was paid to age and rank. Peers and commons treated them as enemies of the English church. Nobody pitied them, and they were bundled off in the bitter night to jail. The feudal church was in the Tower.

How had this great catastrophe come about?

The feudal church consisted of two parts; an English part and a Romish part. Laud and Goodman represented these two parts. Laud wanted to set up an English-popery; Goodman to set up a Romish-popery. Laud counted on the king's support. Goodman counted on the queen's support.

Intent on ousting Laud from his supremacy in church affairs, Goodman had taken a line of opposition which he hoped would bring him, through her majesty's influence, to the front. The time, he thought, had come for throwing off the mask ; for dropping the comedy of English-popery ; and for going in boldly for the popery of Rome. He had observed that Charles, though calling himself an Anglican, was giving his best bishoprics to priests like Wren, late dean of Windsor, who had made themselves acceptable to the queen and her confessor. Wren, 'a Catholic in everything but the name,' had got that see of Hereford which Goodman had unfortunately lost. But Hereford was a second-rate see, and Wren had passed up rapidly from Hereford to Norwich, and from Norwich to Ely. Goodman had proposed to go beyond Laud and Wren in his devotion to the Holy Chair. He had described the church of Rome as 'God's catholic church ; ' he had preached purgatory ; practised auricular confession ; suspended clergymen for denying Rome. Had Father Philip, the queen's confessor, been made a bishop, he could hardly have done more. Goodman's form of faith ran thus :—' I acknowledge Rome to be the mother church.' A bolder priest than either Laud or Wren, he was perfectly willing to accept a cardinal's hat.

When Laud proposed his new Ecclesiastical Canons and Constitutions—by which he swept away the English church as settled in Elizabeth's time—Goodman had refused to sign them; not because they ran so near to Rome, but because they halted at her outer gate. Jealous of so bold a rival, Laud had made an effort to bear him down. The bench was weak; some of the sees being empty, some of the prelates being sick; and Laud had counted on support from Charles. The Canons were as much his work as that of Laud. They brought in English-popery; assigned a ‘sacred’ character to the king; asserted his ‘divine right’ in the state, his ‘supreme power’ in the church. By them, his majesty was proclaimed to be a feudal king and a feudal pope.

Goodman, knowing no pope except the Pope at Rome, had kept aloof, but Laud had pushed him to the wall.

Rising in the synod, and pointing to the Constitutions, Laud had cried aloud:—‘My lord of Gloucester, I admonish you to subscribe.’ Goodman had refused. Rising again, the primate had exclaimed, ‘My lord of Gloucester, I admonish you a second time to subscribe.’ In giving this second warning, Laud had violated rule and custom. Days, if not weeks, had usually interposed between such admonitions. An objector was supposed to need some time for thought, for prayer, and for advice. But Laud, deaf to all voices from the past, had blundered on. Rising once again, he had yelled: 'My lord of Gloucester, I admonish you a third time to subscribe!' Refusing to obey such mandates, Goodman had pleaded conscience. As a bishop, holding his authority from the Holy Spirit, he could only sign as he was moved to sign.

Kindled by this opposition, Laud had proposed to suspend him from his sacred office. Here again, he had been violating rule and custom. Time was needed, notice needed; but no consideration had been strong enough to hold the primate back. Some of the bishops were aghast; yet he had hurried on his course. Turning to Davenant, he had shouted: 'What say you, my lord of Salisbury? Shall my lord of Gloucester be suspended from his office?' Davenant, one of Goodman's comrades, was supposed to share his catholic views. For nineteen years they had lived together in the nest of popery at Windsor; Davenant being chancellor, Goodman canon, of St. George. For that long period they had served at a common altar, met in a common room, and eaten at a common board. Both had known Spalatro, through whom Davenant had derived his apostolic grace. As much a catholic as Goodman, he had been unwilling to desert his colleague. On the primate calling to him again: 'What say you, my lord of Salisbury? Shall my lord of Gloucester be suspended from his office?' he had confessed to feeling scruples. He was not a canonist, he had said, and therefore wished to have the law explained. Two things seemed doubtful to his mind: first, whether the admonitions, to be valid, should not have been given on separate days; second, whether such a synod as that in which they met had full authority to suspend a bishop.

Laud, incensed by his defeat, had hastened to the king, who, in his passion, had sent an officer to arrest the non-subscriber, and to lodge him in the Gate-house. Neither king nor primate had considered, how, in such an act of violence, he was showing the enemies of Episcopacy how they might lay hands on bishops. But the lesson had been quickly caught. If Charles could throw a bishop into jail, why should not Pym?

Laud had been the first to fall. Impeached for setting up his new Constitutions, he had been carried to the Tower, where he was still a prisoner of the crown. Wren had followed Laud. Like every man who had lived at Windsor, in the atmosphere poisoned by Spalatro, Wren was suspected and abhorred. A cry had risen against him in his diocese, which he was said to have converted into a common jail. Arrested as a papist in disguise, he had been committed to the Tower. These acts had been followed by the scene of yesterday, when a majority of their brethren were compelled to kneel at the bar, to answer charges of high treason, and to have their bail refused.

The bishops were the king's martyrs; for their main offence was that of having declared his order 'sacred' and his right 'divine.'

Monday, January 24th.

The day of trial came, and was postponed. Meantime a bill was pushed through both the Houses for abolishing episcopacy at a blow. Charles had a great repugnance to this bill. 'No bishops, no king!' had been his father's cry; and he had got the principle in his heart. If bishops fell, he feared the throne would fall. This bill, the Root and Branch bill, was before the peers. All those who loved the king, all those who loved the bishops, were entreated by his majesty to resist.

Richmond, his Papist kinsman, gave expression to his ire by hinting that the House had better adjourn for six months. His levity cost him dear. He was enjoined to kneel at the bar, withdraw his words, and humbly ask forgiveness of his peers. The House of Commons wished to have him banished from the court. Few cared to join in battle for the bench. Many of those who stood by Charles were willing to abandon Laud and Goodman. On the eve of rising, Digby had said: 'No people have ever been provoked more than the generality of England in late years, by the insolence of these prelates.' Falkland declared that those who hated bishops, hated them like the devil, while those who liked them most would not lose a dinner to save their lives.

Friday, February 5th.

Messengers, spurring in hot haste, brought word to Charles that the bishops' bill had passed the third reading in the House of Peers, and would be sent to him on Monday for his signature. Three bishops had protested, but no lay peer had joined them in their protest. In the hour of trial, episcopacy, rooted in the soil for upwards of a thousand years, had hardly found a friend. Here were the fruits of Laud's English - popery and Goodman's Romish - popery. When episcopacy became confounded with popery, episcopacy was doomed.

On Monday, Craven and Monmouth came to Windsor with the bill, and craved his majesty's assent. It was a popular bill, as they could testify. On Saturday, when the news got out that it had passed through parliament, bonfires had been lit in every street, and all the parish bells had been rung, as on the news of some great victory. Next day, the churches had been filled, and everyone had hailed the birth of a new time.

In eight days it would come into force; therefore he was desired to sign at once.

Charles turned away. Put down his bishops— the supporters of his throne—clothed in their apostolic grace! He asked for time. He must consult his council. It was utterly against his conscience to comply. Could he not satisfy the peers some other way? On other points he was disposed to yield. Suppose he pardoned Mandeville; suppose he stayed his accusation of the Five Members? There was hardly anything he would refuse, if he might save his bishops from that fall. Craven and Monmouth pressed their bill Of his three councillors, Hyde was for resistance, Falkland for gaining time, Culpepper for assent. Culpepper was at Windsor when the news came in. 'It must be done, your majesty,' was Culpepper's advice. 'Is that Ned Hyde's opinion?' asked the king. 'No, sir,' replied the councillor. 'Then I am of Ned Hyde's opinion, and will run the hazard.'

Craven and Monmouth pressed their errand. It was but a form they asked. A week hence, the provisions of their bill would be in force. The king held out a few days longer, till the Lords, assisted by Culpepper, found means to act on his majesty's fears.

Defeated by parliament, the English and the Romish prelates lay in the Tower awaiting trial for high treason.

The Stuarts had achieved their sacred miracle :— in less than forty years they had turned the hearts of Englishmen against their church.

CHAPTER XVIII.

PARLEYING.

1642.

DIGBY's campaign was over in a week. One Thursday he had quitted Windsor, to commence his war for the deliverance of king and queen; the following Thursday he was housed, under a false name, 'in the privatest way,' at the Golden Fleece—a tavern in the market-place of Middelburg, in the Isle of Walcheren. The free companies that were to have crushed the city bands, and pitched the king's enemies into the Thames, had broken and dispersed. Their leader was a fugitive, waiting for fresh 'instructions' at the Golden Fleece.

Suspicion followed him to his hiding-place. Before his failure in the field, he had become intensely irksome to his peers, whom he had equally insulted and deceived. ' This is no free Parliament,' he had sneered ; but he had instantly been made to lower that tone. 'My wife is sick at Sherbourne, and I crave permission to bring her up,' had been the lie by which he gained his leave of absence from their lordships' House. Before he drew the sword, he was known to be intimate with the queen. A catholic, more or less concealed — a favourite with the Capuchins and bedchamber women — he was suspected, with good reason, to have been the bad adviser who had led her majesty to insist on prosecuting Mandeville and the Five Members. No one pitied him in his fall. Proclaimed a traitor, he was summoned to attend the House. His horses, arms, and properties, were seized; his servants were arrested, searched, and given in charge. When it was known that he had made his escape in a royal ship, Pennington, the king's admiral in the narrow seas, was ordered to attend the bar. A watch was set at Flushing, and about the Golden Fleece. Digby was sure to write to Windsor; orders were given that his expresses should be stopped and his packets seized.

For some days darkness and confusion fell on the royal house. Unnerved by failure on all sides, Charles was disposed to parley with his enemies; the course lay open if he chose to ask for terms.

Digby's rising was not laid to his account. Where nothing had been signed, little could be proved—even if anybody in his senses had wished for proof. Charles was aware that no one wished to rake up evidence against him. He was king—royal, if not sacred—and surrounded by a halo of respect. No party leader dreamt as yet of touching the regal office. In the eyes of every one the regal office was an appanage of the English race. England was royal. If kingly rule were not invented by the race, it was an emblem of their legendary and historic rights. With them ' the king never dies.' Most of the ancient English laws and liberties were connected with the names of kings ; the franchises of Alfred and the laws of Edward the Confessor being the pride of every English heart. Kings might be good or bad, yet no personal weakness, no personal wickedness, had disturbed the virtues of the English crown. What changes were in store, no man could tell ; but for the day, no party leader was prepared to rake up evidence against the crown. A minister might be struck, a primate lodged in jail, but no one dreamt as yet of aiming at the king and queen.

One day, while Digby was at sea, and nothing had been heard about him, the queen pretended to take fright. The Commons, she declared, were making articles against her. She was thrown into a state of bodily fear. To Newport, when he came to Windsor with official papers, she not only told this story, but produced a copy of the articles. Her object may have been to frighten Charles, and stop his wish to parley; or she may have simply wished to try the ground beneath her feet. She knew what mischief she had done, and what the leaders in the country thought of her. To catholics she might seem to be Clothilde, but in the eyes of knights and burgesses she was Jezebel. A comedy had been lately played between them. She was ailing, she had said, and thought of going abroad. Twice in her younger days, the waters at Spa had done her good; she had a mind to drink those waters in her present state. The Commons, having their suspicions, had desired to know what ailed her, and had ordered Mayerne to report—first, on the queen's complaint, and second, on the medicinal properties of the springs at Spa. ' Nerves,' he had said; ' disorder of the mind,' on which the Commons had suggested that the disorder in her majesty's ' nerves ' might be cured by an agreement of the king and state, which she might greatly help them to bring about.

On hearing of her pretended scare, the Commons prayed the Lords to send some peer to Windsor, and induce her majesty to disclose the name of her informant. No such articles had been prepared ; no such articles had been proposed. Some mischief-maker had deceived the queen. Let her give up his name, that they might punish him for spreading false reports. Newport and Seymour were despatched to Windsor, but her majesty had no one to give up. It was a rumour, she had heard, and nothing more. Articles of impeachment! She had heard of articles, but had never seen them. The affair was so unlikely, she had given no heed to the report. Finding the House had never taken such a course, she was content. She never meant to accuse a single peer. How, then, should she accuse a House of Peers?

The comedy was played. Her ailments, mineral springs, and articles of impeachment, were allowed to drop.

Parleying went on. Falkland, Secretary of State, came over, and was closeted with Charles. Wise, tolerant, popular, Falkland was the man to save him, if by any chance he could yet be saved. His majesty smiled and bowed, and yielded, to the outer eye, on many points. He posed himself before Falkland as he posed himself before Vandyck. Day after day his words grew smoother and his promises fairer. He was ready, he asserted, to forget the past ; to drop his accusations, to accept advice, and even to confess his faults. In some things he had been misled ; men whom he trusted had betrayed his confidence, but these mistakes, now seen in their true light, could be repaired. All that was wanting was the spirit, on both sides, to forgive and to forget. ' Whatever mistaking had grown in the government, either of Church or State, might be removed, and all things reduced to the order of the time of Queen Elizabeth—the memory whereof is justly precious to this nation:'—such were his words. Had he possessed the virtue and the strength to travel on that line, the dynasty might have been saved.

Another storm broke out.

Digby wrote from the Golden Fleece ; his letters, taken on the road to Windsor, were perused by Pym. One letter bore her majesty's address, and proved that she was privy to his plots. He asked for orders and a cypher ; hinted at the matters which had failed, and at the policy to be still pursued. He named the terms on which he would venture to return. ' If the king betake himself to a safe place, where he may avow and protect his servants, . . . I shall then live in impatience and in misery till I wait upon you. But if — after all he hath done of late — he shall betake himself to the easiest and compliantest ways of accommodation, I am confident that then I shall serve him more by my absence than by all my industry.'

The queen was hot for war; a war that should be open and avowed. Why had they failed? Because their war was unavowed. Nobody knew how far he had a right to go. Take Goring; he was pledged to her, yet when the moment came, he had done nothing. Hundreds of officers were in Goring's shoes; sworn to her service, yet unable to strike a blow. Must all that she had done be thrown aside? She had engaged a host of partizans; she had laid her hands on the Crown jewels. These were advantages not to be flung away.

Charles still wavered in his mind. One day he listened to the queen, and felt her fiery breath sweep through his soul; next day, he listened to

the Secretary, and talked of riding down to Westminster, and making terms of peace.

The queen was rich in plans. She offered to
cross the sea, to carry off the Crown jewels, and
make a new attempt to carry off the prince.
Charles, as Digby had suggested, should retire on
a strong place, farther from the capital than
Windsor. There, he should raise the royal flag,
and call his people under arms. Men, arms, and
money, would come in. At Rotterdam, she could
sell the jewels, take up ships, raise companies, and
return to help him with a fleet and army. Sailing
under lawful colours, and receiving lawful pay,
his crews and troops would know how to defend
their king.

Listening to her voice, he felt inclined to go
with her — the Clothilde of her race and faith.
When left alone, he pondered on the risk, not only
to his life, but to his crown. All power seemed
slipping from his hands. His bishops were in
jail, his officers were insulted and condemned, his
fortresses were no longer his; Constable and
Chamberlain refused to come when he required
them. He was barely master of his Castle-gates.
How, if he kept his course, was he to hold his

own? It was impossible. He must go back; he must undo what he had done, and let his people have what they desired—Elizabeth's kingdom and Elizabeth's church.

This yielding mood provoked her majesty to scorn. Give up his cause? Why so? He was still a king. Only one officer had failed. Thousands were ready to take his place. England lay open to his enterprise. Let him retire from Windsor. A hundred miles from London, he could raise his flag, and issue an appeal. Then he would see. The tempest of her passion drove him on, and finally he agreed with her to fight.

The first thing was to get the queen away from Windsor; she and the Crown jewels, which she had to pawn or sell. Mary's betrothal to the Prince of Orange furnished an excuse. The bridegroom pressed to have his bride; the queen proposed to take her to the Hague. It was not easy to refuse her, and the peers were glad to have the court away from Windsor; but they sent off Capel and Portland to require the king's assent to the bishops' bill before the queen set out. That bill, they were to hint, must be adopted ere the roads to Dover could be guaranteed. Culpepper lent his help. Seeking the queen, he urged her to intercede with Charles. Her fears might overcome a scruple which resisted sage advice. The queen fell in with his design. She was unwilling to be stopt, and more unwilling to be searched. A word from her and all was done; before they passed the gates, the king agreed to sign.

His reign at Windsor lasted just four weeks. Coming on Wednesday, he left on Wednesday; but in that interval he had fallen from the height of a king to that of a pretender. He was more than half dethroned. His sovereign rights were gone. His bishops were deposed. He was no longer master of his house. A rival power disputed his control of fortresses and ports. One course, and only one, lay open to him — an appeal to arms. He came to Windsor for a private war; he left, to tempt his fortune in a public war. He put his crown and life at stake. He threw his kingly office in the scale against his country's right.

On which side was the strength of England to be found? A hundred battle-fields had to reply. Till that debate was over, Charles was never to re-enter the royal house.

CHAPTER XIX.

ROUNDHEADS.

1672.

Tap, tap! over heath and holt came the sound of Roundhead drums—of steadily advancing Roundhead drums; unpleasant music in the ears of Aminadab Harrison and his merry men. Order, even in disorder, was a principle of the men in power at Westminster. No Robin Hoods were henceforth needed in defence of popular rights. When Charles retired from Windsor, his feudal system vanished, and the park and forest fell into possession of the state—as trustee for the crown.

As Charles rode out, his Constable rode in; not in obedience to a royal summons, but to that of an order from his peers. As Ranger of the park, his duty called him to the keep. He was to warn the rioters to disperse; if they resisted, to arrest and bring them up to Westminster. But he was no more fortunate than before. Aminadab laughed him in the face; on which he threatened and retired. Finding an open field before them, the intruders grew in numbers, till the noise of their misdoings rivalled the tumult of a royal hunt.

Holland, too weak to cope with them, reported to his peers. A body of rustics, living in the villages round Windsor, had got possession of the park and forest; gathering 'in a riotous and tumultuous manner,' they defied his orders, beat his keepers, and killed his majesty's deer. More than a hundred fallow-deer had been slain and stolen. Nor were the marauders satisfied with hunting in the forest; they had broken down his fences, and had threatened to destroy his lodge. The uproar caused by them could be heard in the King's house. 'Send for the sheriff; let him answer for the peace,' the Lords replied in practical orders; and, within a month, Robin Hood and Little John, otherwise Aminadab Harrison and John Patey, had been taken prisoners, brought to Westminster, found guilty of trespass, and returned to Berks, under sentence of imprisonment in the county jail with hard labour, till the pleasure of the Lords should be further shown.

But park and chase were not yet cleared. In

forty years, a generation of rustics had grown up in license, with the feeling of their class entirely on their side, and that of the better sort partially on their side. Tramps, deer-stealers, and intruders of all sorts, were slow to understand the change. Here stretched the king's park, there skipped the king's deer:—why, were they not to enter and to take their own as they had done for many a year? Unable to read the new rules, they went on snaring deer and carrying off lops and tops. Again the Constable reported to his peers. Considering it 'a blemish to government, to deface his majesty's parks and forests,' the Lords invited Mandeville to assist the Constable in restoring peace. Some of the thieves were caught and caged; but the disorder, bred in the bone of tramp and poacher, was not easily suppressed.

Tap, tap! the Roundhead drums were heard; a tramp of many feet, with Venn, the city captain, in their front. John Venn, a mercer in Cheapside, and a member for the city, had a name among the companies only second to Skippon, under whom he had drilled and served. Venn was a typical man. Bold, talkative, unabashed, he had been equally useful to his party in the House and in the street. He liked to rail against the king; to rustle and insult the guard. More than once he marched his company down to Westminster in defiance of the king and of his troop. A gospeller like himself, his wife was no less ardent in the cause. One day, during a debate, he sent to her a scrawl. The cause, he said, was going ill; bad men were having their own way; he could not leave the House. Could she contrive to send some help? Running from house to house, she stirred up friends, got them under way, and marched with them to Westminster, where they arrived in the nick of time.

Raised to the rank of colonel, Venn set out for Windsor at the head of twelve companies of foot. He was to seize the Castle, strengthen the defences, and to hold the post as governor, in the name of king and parliament. Blood was already flowing in the west, and troops were moving from the north towards London. Essex, the new Lord-General, saw the value of Windsor as a fore-post and defence of the metropolis. But Windsor was a good deal more to Essex than a fore-post and defence. To all men, Windsor was still royal, and to some she was sacred: the depository of their national sentiment. She seemed the natural head-quarters of a country under arms. She was an answer and denial to a court set up elsewhere. He who held Windsor seemed as though he held the crown.

Both sides were soon of this opinion, and to both sides Windsor became an object of desire.

After seeing his wife embark, Charles, acting on Digby's plan, rode up into the north; into those shires which held on doggedly to the ancient ways, and had no fear of any number of returning Cardinal Poles. At York, he ousted Essex from his post of Chamberlain; and invested Lindsay with the staff. It was an act of warfare. Lindsay was a soldier who had served with Essex on the Rhine. At parting from his consort, Charles had promised her he would draw the sword, call up the country, march on London, and destroy the city bands. She took his pledge that he would never enter London till he rode in as a conqueror at the head of his victorious troops. Lindsay, the new Chamberlain, was named Lord-General of his forces, with Prince Rupert as his Master of the Horse. In answer to this challenge, Essex was named Lord-General of the popular bands. 'Hey for Robin!' shouted the volunteers. He was so popular in the city, that an army sprang up at his call. 'Without him,' said the royalists, 'they would hardly have been able to raise a regiment.' Essex and Lindsay, formerly comrades on the Rhine, now faced each other; Essex on the Thames, and Lindsay on the Ouse.

Digby crept over with a message from the queen. Arms, men, and money, he assured his majesty, were on board. The queen was moving heaven and earth in his behalf; here, kneeling with her monks, there, haggling with her Jews. But Digby, coming in disguise, and only seeing the king by stealth, was far from satisfied with the aspect of affairs. The king lay too far north; and seemed to be a fugitive from his realm. Instead of throwing off his mask and mingling with the court, he took his leave, with two or three bed-chamber men, and crept back towards the coast.

Weeks later on, two armies, slowly formed and poorly trained, met near Edge Hill—drew blood—and then fell back ; the cavaliers retiring on Oxford, the roundheads on Warwick ; neither side much weakened by the fray. Edge Hill was fought on Sunday afternoon. Early in the day, while service was proceeding in St. George's chapel, Captain Fog, a roundhead officer, appeared at Windsor, and demanded from the dean and canons the key of their strong-room. His orders were, to take away their plate. The dean, Christopher Wren, a brother of the culprit in the Tower, took fright; for Fog was bold of face, and help, in his distress, seemed far away. He tried to gain a little time. Three keys, he said, were needed to unlock the door; these keys were held by different persons, who were not in residence that day. Fog called in blacksmiths, who, with crow-bars, smashed the stone jambs, and made a way into their strong-room. Fog took away the plate; rods, basons, flagons, candlesticks, all solid silver, chased by Nüremberg artists, and triple gilt. Much 'papistry' was noted on that college plate; legends of Moses and the tables, David and the Ark, angels of incense, and figures touching for the king's evil. Fog carried all away, and his employers dropped that superstition into the roundhead melting-pots.

On Friday, five days later, Venn arrived, and took up his abode as governor in St. George's keep. He had not come one day too soon. The king, finding himself nearer to London than his enemy, descended by the Thames valley, meaning to move on Westminster, and to regain the royal house. At Maidenhead, Rupert turned off towards Windsor, but the roundhead companies were in strong possession of the gates and towers. A castle on a height, defended by artillery, is not a place to be assailed by troops of horse, armed with nothing but swords and carbines. Burning with rage, Rupert drew off, and spurred to Colnbrook, where his uncle lay in strength, already, as he thought, the master of his capital.

Some of the citizens, urged by panic, were inclined to sue for terms. On what terms would his majesty be pleased to treat? Retire from Windsor, was the king's reply. If they desired to treat, he would reside at Windsor till the articles were signed. But Venn and his companies must vacate the royal house. Some of the leaders were inclined to yield, but a majority clung to the idea of retaining Windsor till the articles were signed. Would Charles agree? Pembroke and Northumberland rode out to Colnbrook, in the hope of persuading him to lie at Reading and Maidenhead, leaving the Castle in the hands of Venn. He was unwilling to accept such terms; Windsor was his house; Venn had no business there. While they were parleying over Windsor, Essex came up. By throwing troops into Acton, Brentford, and Kingston, he sealed up every road from Colnbrook to the capital. Charles, shut out alike from Westminster and Windsor, agreed to hold his ground and negotiate from his actual camp.

But Rupert, chafing at these delays, and eager to cut his way through the roundhead lines, dashed forward, contrary to the truce, surprised the companies at Brentford, and drove them out; but with such loss of men and horses as prevented him advancing on the London road. On hearing of this outrage, Essex joined his troops, brought out the city bands, and pushed the cavaliers back from Brentford, through their former lines at Colnbrook, into Maidenhead and Reading.

Windsor was no longer menaced by the king. But Essex, finding the place of so much value, took up his abode in the royal house; fixing his head-quarters in the town and on St. George's keep.

Leaving a garrison at Reading, Charles fell back on Oxford, which became his own head-quarters for the war. Thus, at the end of one campaign, Windsor and Oxford were entrenched against each other; each the head-quarters of a hostile camp and cause.

CHAPTER XX.

CAVALIER PRISONERS.

1643.

In the chief apartment of the Norman tower may still be read this scrap of personal history in stone:

Sir Edmund Fortescue,

Prisoner in this Chamber,

12 day January, 1642.

This date is in the old style; Sir Edmund scratched his name on his prison wall on the twelfth day of January, 1643.

Sir Edmund Fortescue was an early victim of the shibboleth—'King or Parliament?' It was a query hard for men to answer, even when put to them in their cooler moments. Seven men in ten throughout the nation were for king *and* parliament; and a heavy burden lay on those who drove them into choosing sides. Here lay the pathos of those times, when happy homes were broken up, and families rent in twain by passions kindled at a distance from the domestic hearth. Fortescue was brought to Windsor in a batch of fifty-five prisoners, all of them taken on the field of battle, urging their cause with sword and pike. Sir Francis Dodington, Sir John Smith, and Sir William Valentine, were in the batch—each stolen away from wife and child, from pleasant home, yule-logs, and Christmas holidays. Some of the fifty-five were sheriffs of their counties ; others were burgesses of the county towns. At home, and even in Westminster, the parties had a common cry : 'Crown, religion, parliament.' It was only in the field, with loaded piece and pointed lance, that either disputant put his question plainly : King or parliament ? Fortescue and his fellows were received at Windsor in the king's name, as culprits taken in the fact of levying war against the king !

Though Essex and his staff held the King's house, Venn was Governor of the Castle, and to him the captives were consigned.

During the Christmas holidays, parliament grew conscious of the fact, that fighting leads to prisoners being taken; also to the fact that prisoners, on surrender, must be housed and watched. No preparations had been made to lodge them. Those who came in first were welcomed, and the ordinary jails sufficed: their coming was a public sight, an evidence of success in action; but the Clinke and Fleet, the Comptors and King's Bench, were quickly filled. Prisoners kept pouring in; on which the managers of the war, with crafty humour, seized the bishops' palaces, and turned them into common jails. Laud was in the Tower: why not use the chambers of Lambeth house? Wren was in the Tower: why not use the chambers of Ely house? Juxon and Curle were absent: why not use the chambers of London house and Winchester house? When all these piles were choked with prisoners, the authorities turned towards Windsor. Space, they saw, might be secured in St. George's keep, the Norman tower, the Outer gate, and in the Poor Knights' tenements. Should more space be needed, they might clear the nest, driving out dean and canons, servitors and singing-men. Thus fifty-five cavalier gentlemen were removed to Windsor, chiefly from the King's Bench and from Winchester house.

On entering, every man had to pay his fee,

according to his rank; an ensign or lieutenant, twenty-six shillings and eightpence; a knight, captain, or esquire, forty shillings; a colonel, or man of quality, sixty-six shillings and eightpence. Venn allotted them such rooms as he saw fit, such as their means allowed them to keep up. As yet the prison rules were mild, the strife being still regarded as a neighbours' strife, soon to be healed again. A prisoner was allowed to bring in food and fuel. When they first arrived the rooms were empty, having neither tables, chairs, nor beds; but all these things were soon supplied. A prisoner had the freedom of his ward; no stranger was allowed to speak with him, but he was free to move about and to enjoy the prospect from his wall or tower. All letters had to pass under Venn's eye; but where no public matters were discussed they were at once distributed to his guests. No harshness in the rule, no violence in the jailer, stained this period of the war.

Fortescue and Dodington chose to lodge in the Norman tower—the rooms in which Surrey had lived and sung.

Fortescue was thirty-two years old, a man of handsome person, with a cavalier's locks about his neck, and small moustache and tuft, worn in

the fashion patronised by his prince. The family
seat was Fallapit, in Devonshire, a charming nook
on a charming country side. There lived his
father, John Fortescue, a hale but aged western
squire. Sir Edmund was high sheriff. All members of the family were cavaliers ; his father, and
his brother Peter, being no less ardent than himself.
Lady Fortescue went with him heart and soul.
When Hertford, casting in his lot with Charles,
appeared in Somerset and called his tenants under
arms, Fortescue began to move in Devonshire; but
Bedford, sent into the western shires, drove Hertford back, and kept the royalists of Devonshire in
check. Not until Hopton came, was Fortescue able
to array his county bands. Then he moved out,
his father and his brother joining him in the field.
At Modbury they encountered Ruthven, and a
flying roundhead corps, who broke their lines, and
drove them into headlong flight. His band dispersed, the sheriff made for Champernoun house,
a strong place, which he hoped to hold against his
enemy. His father and his brother followed him.

Ruthven was a soldier, and he pushed the
fugitive so sternly that the volunteers laid down
their swords. Champernoun and the Fortescues
were put on board a ship, and brought by sea to

Gravesend, whence forty pikemen marched them up to Southwark, and dispersed them into several jails. Sir Edmund and his father were lodged in Winchester house, so that the old man might be comforted by his son. Champernoun and Peter Fortescue were placed in the King's Bench. The sheriff was then sent to Windsor; but his brother Peter was allowed to take his place at his father's side. The charities of civil life were not yet scotched away by the consuming fire of civil war.

The sheriff stayed eight months in the Norman tower. Hopton had gained advantages for the king, and many roundhead officers were in his hands. Sir Edmund, with his father and his brother, was exchanged. He went back to his home; but he had tasted blood, and the delights of home soon palled on his excited spirit. He raised a company, marched on Salcombe, and raised a strong work there, which he called Fort Charles. This post he held a long time, and only yielded when the war was almost at an end. On giving his word to live abroad, he was allowed to cross sea. He made for Delft; but he had spent his force, and in the following year he died.

Not far from Fortescue's inscription may be

read this second scrap of personal history in stone:

DODINGTON.

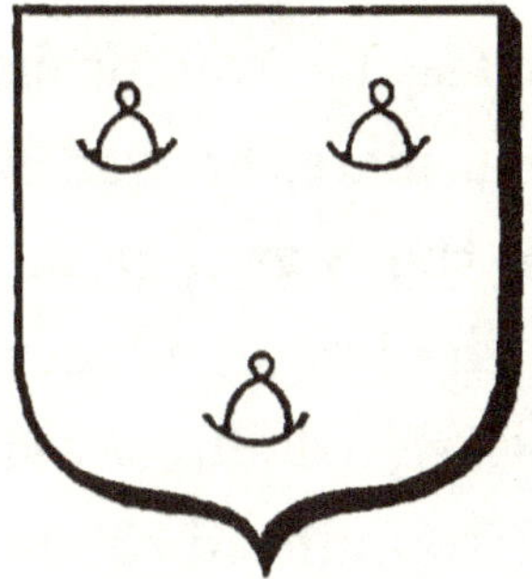

Sir Francis Dodington was, like Fortescue, a western man, and his appeal to arms, like that of Fortescue, was the rending of a happy home. Born and bred in Somerset, in the hamlet from which he derived his name, he had never drawn his sword in anger till the war broke out. Then had been put to him, as of all Englishmen of age to carry arms, the query: King or parliament? He answered 'King.' John, his eldest son, refused. Lady Dodington was dead. Father and son were parted on the hearthstone. John stood out for parliament. When Hertford came into the west, Sir Francis joined him, and displayed such energy in the cause as made him, like his neighbour, Robert Blake, a name of fear to the opposing side ; but unlike Blake, he had the misery of being captured at an early date, and sharing Fortescue's imprisonment in the Norman tower.

How long he lay at Windsor is uncertain. Like the Fortescues, he was probably exchanged ; and, like his room-mate, he was hardly free before he plunged into the war again. Few men did better service to the king. One rattling brush he had with Major Carr, which saved a royal convoy from a troop of roundhead horse. But all his strength was spent in vain. Like others of his quality and fortune, he observed the king's decline with sorrowing heart. His soul was in the cause. His home, his son, were nothing in the scale. When all was over with his master, all was over with himself. Stealing away to France, he roamed from place to place, living a vagrant life, forgotten by his friends, and earning a little bread by the sale of English knives. Yet in his lowest fortunes he retained his handsome person and his courtly air. A lady, who was giving him food and clothes for charity, struck by his manner, kept him in her house, inquired into his history, and finding him a gentleman, became his wife. Thus life began for him again. Two sons were born to him of this foreign match. John, his first-born by his

English wife, had entered into Cromwell's service, and become the secretary of his minister, Thurloe. The fugitive knew him not. The two French boys he reared as soldiers, and he placed them in the army of his adopted prince.

In old age, under a second Charles, the wanderer appeared at Dodington. His side was up; his son's was down. No one objected to his entering on his own. The best of his estate was gone; yet he disdained to speak of recompense. At length he passed into the land of dreams, leaving this record in this name and shield, carved on his prison-wall in the Norman tower.

CHAPTER XXI.

HEAD-QUARTERS.

1643-5.

Essex lay at Windsor till the spring. During the winter months, parley was going on with Charles, who kept his court at Oxford, though his heart was in the royal house. In every note, from Oxford to Westminster, the name turned up. Charles wanted to regain his house and keep. Much of the country was in his possession. Reading he held in strength. A good deal of Berks, still more of Bucks, lay under his control. He had an army at his back, and might re-enter Windsor with the pomp and glory of a king. When he had left, a year ago, he had neither men nor guns; none of the force that gilds and deepens the halo round a royal head. Now, he was strong enough to avow his policy and defend his cause. At Windsor, his position would be safe.

The lords with whom he parleyed, were as firm in holding to the royal house. 'His majesty's forces shall advance no nearer to Windsor than Wheatly,' six miles from Oxford, was their first demand, when offering terms of truce. A line, twelve miles round Windsor, might be drawn, and they would keep within that line if Charles would draw a similar line round Oxford, and agree to take no ground beyond that line.

But Charles refused. He counted on the magic of his name and on the disposition of his peers. Pembroke was preaching peace. Bedford and Holland were preparing to desert their flag. Why not Essex and the men at Windsor? In the rush of horse at Edge Hill, a roundhead colonel had come over. Other colonels were suspected of a wish to follow suit. Since Charles left Windsor, the situation had completely changed. In other days, Charles was the innovator, both in church and state. His bishops and his ministers were odious in the sight of moderate men. Now, he was a conservative; willing to go back on church and state as they had stood in Queen Elizabeth's time. His enemies had become the innovators, both in church and state. So far from being satisfied with an English church and an English state,

the leaders were hankering after foreign models,—
a Genevan theocracy, a Munster commonwealth.
Piqued by such vagaries, ordinary men were turning once more in weariness towards the crown.

Were Essex gained and Windsor occupied for
the king, Charles might be strong enough to
fix his own terms of peace. Could Essex be
seduced? Charles thought so. Essex showed no
zeal. A captain, skilled in war, he stood in harness,
but he threw no heart into the work. A peer, with
large estates and torpid views, he wanted no
material change. To go back on the settlements of
Elizabeth was enough for him, and for every person of his class. In joining the reformers, he was
helping to resist innovation. He had hardly
dreamed of war, and never of a war against the
crown. 'For king and parliament!' was his daily
cry. To raise his point against the king was no
less a crime than sacrilege. At Edge Hill, his aim
was rescue—nothing more; an effort to deliver
Charles from the society of his evil councillors.
Step by step, he had been led into a false position,
till he found himself at Windsor, at the head of a
rebel army, which denied the king admittance to
the royal house.

A letter came to him from Oxford. Charles,

assuring him of forgiveness of the past, entreated him to put an end to the unhappy strife. It lay with Essex. Charles was ready to conclude a truce and to confer with him on terms of peace. Let Essex say the word, and peace might be secured.

Essex was aware of his position. Some of the fanatics were already railing at him. He was tender to the king—averse to hitting hard, afraid of shedding blood. Voices in the rear were calling out for a new general; one who would lay on and spare not, till their enemies were smitten hip and thigh. These railers galled him; but the day was not yet come when he could walk with them no more.

He answered: that he tendered his services at the royal feet, and was willing to hazard his life and fortune in his majesty's defence; that from the beginning of these troubles he had worked for peace; that he had a great trust laid on him for the defence of his majesty's person, God's true religion, and the public good; and that his conscience bound him to discharge that trust. Should that trust be taken from him and bestowed on a worthier man, he would not only give it up, but hold himself in readiness to save his majesty against any of his foreign enemies.

Here the correspondence dropt, and Essex drew his forces round the Castle for the spring campaign.

A bridge was built by Venn. A Windsor regiment was raised, and many a bout of wine was held at the White Hart, between the roundhead mayor and Colonel Venn. The royal garrison at Reading plagued the district; and the general laid his plans for marching on that town; but his regiments were not yet strong enough in numbers nor inured enough to discipline for serious work. Windsor had been their Capua.

Neither Essex nor Venn had full control over the park and forest; and the soldiers, having arms and fellowship, were far more troublesome than Aminadab's merry men. Sprung from the lower ranks, they had a fellow-feeling with the park-breakers and deer-stealers. Stationed in the town, they roamed about the park, and helped themselves to venison and wood. Complaints arose. A keeper swore that the Lord-General's soldiers crashed into the park, threw down the stakes, and killed the stags and deer—more than five hundred stags and deer. One keeper tried to stop a soldier who was doing mischief, and the soldier killed him on the spot. Of all marauders in the park, his lordship's troops had proved the worst. Holland could do nothing—Essex could do little—to prevent their violence. Some outside rascals, taken in the fact, were clapt in jail; but troops and regiments packing for the march and siege were not to be broken for the sake of dead deer, much less for the sake of charred rails. What could be safely done, was done. Ten days before Essex struck his tents, the House of Lords took the Great park under their special care.

The general gone, Venn broke into the deanery and the college. Who were these fellows, idling in the inn-yard, when the day of toil had come?' 'Clerks and minor canons,' they replied. 'Then join the standard,' answered Venn; 'go forth and fight for king and parliament.' They claimed exemption, being men of peace and servants of the church. To take up arms was contrary to their consciences. 'Troop out, then!' cried the military mercer, and the servitors of the chapel had to troop.

The Lords were shocked; but men like Venn were coming to the top. Mandeville, now earl of Manchester, and speaker in the House of Lords, warned him to take care of St. George's chapel; to see that the registers and monuments of the order were preserved. He was required to leave the college men to their rooms, so long as they kept the peace. But Venn took little heed of Manchester. His party were advancing to the front; men of Testwood's stamp, to whom saints were popery, and effigies only dust. Essex had hardly quitted Reading on his way towards Oxford, when this roundhead strode into the choir, pulled down the shields and hangings, took away the plate and ornaments, and then robbed the tombs of their gold and jewels. Venn had no respect for saints—even for a national saint.

A year passed by, with fifty battles and no results.

The queen came back, with men and money, to resume her sway and to ruin Charles; who not only followed her advice, but called in witnesses to see how thoroughly he had become her slave. From that hour, neutral men fell off, leaving the papists and the sectaries to fight their fight. Victory turned from side to side. Waller defeated Herbert near Gloucester; Newcastle beat Fairfax at Bramham Moor. Essex took Reading; Hopton routed Stamford. Goring was taken at Wakefield; Rupert gained an advantage at Chalgrove. Hampden fell; and then Falkland fell. Essex cleared the field at

Newbury; Waller lost the day on Roundway Down. Essex returned to Windsor; Charles returned to Oxford :—nothing had been achieved.

One day, a trumpeter came to the Castle gates from Oxford, with a packet for the Lord-General. Essex bore that packet, unopened, to the House of Lords. He had grown afraid of snares. A second year of war had multiplied his critics, who were crying out, and louder than before, that he spared the king. Bedford and Holland had gone over. Many suspected him of a design to follow suit. His frankness saved him—for a time. The message proved to be a fresh appeal to him for peace; but peace to be arranged between Oxford and Windsor, in which the Lords and Commons were to have no part. 'Let the Lord-General write to him, since *we* are not addressed,' was the reply of parliament. Brief and stern were the Lord-General's words. He and his friends, he told the king, had armed to uphold the rights of parliament, and were resolved to spend their lives in vindication of those rights, as being the foundation on which all their laws and liberties were built.

In May, next year, Essex marched from Windsor with the roundhead army for his third and last campaign. Turning on Oxford, he edged the royalist forces towards the west. Charles fell back on Exeter; the queen crossed over into France. Yet weeks dragged on, and hardly anything was done. Again the cry arose that Charles was being spared; again the cry was raised in favour of a change. Paston, pretending to see signs and visions, interfered with officers, and made appeals against those officers to the rank and file. Dissensions rent the camps. Waller, a subtle and ambitious general, sided with the sectaries and disobeyed his chief's commands. Essex lost heart; and being entangled in a difficult country, stept on board a boat, and left his column to dissolve. His horse broke through; his infantry made terms. That great roundhead army was to rally on the Windsor grass no more.

The roundhead troops had come to have opinions; and an army that has more than one opinion is a Mob.

Windsor remained head-quarters; but a new general was to lodge in the King's house, a new army, founded on a new principle, to gather round the Windsor slopes.

CHAPTER XXII.

THE NEW MODEL.

1645.

THE new general was Fairfax : the new army was a sect.

On reaching Windsor, Fairfax met his first regiment of horse, composed of men whom Cromwell had raised and trained, and who had recently flashed and stormed over the field at Marston Moor. 'We charged their regiments of foot with our horse, and routed all we charged. God made them stubble to our swords.' These men were picketed in the town and under the Castle wall ; models, on whose strong and steady lines he was to form his troops and regiments for the next campaign.

A son of Ferdinando, Lord Fairfax of Cameron, the new Lord-General came of a strong-headed and quick-hitting race, long settled on the Yorkshire moors. Some of the family had been bailiffs, reeves, and sheriffs; but the chiefs had been mostly fighting-men, loving the sword and saddle as the weapon and the seat of a hardy stock. One of the house had helped in the sack of Rome. Most of the males had been knighted on the field. To prove their grit, they had drunk and fought with almost equal ardour, and more than once had been only saved from ruin, by their luck in attracting wealthy girls. One of the family had given himself up to verse; but the translator of Tasso into English had been an illegitimate son. No genuine Fairfax could have any other passion than the saddle and the sword. Thomas, the first lord, had seen sharp service on the Rhine. One of his sons had found a soldier's grave in Turkey; and a second had fallen, sword in hand, at the gates of Montauban. Two others had been slain at Frankenthal. Ferdinando, the second lord, had been one of the first men in Yorkshire to rise against the king. As colonel of the York bands, general of the West Riding, governor of Hull, and commander in the north, he had been the leader in a dozen fights.

Tom, the son of that second lord, had been early sent into foreign camps to learn the family trade. Leaving Cambridge at sixteen, he had taken service under Vere, from whom he learnt his first lesson in the art of war, and to whom he had made his first engagement in the court of love. Vere's religion had become his faith; Vere's daughter had become his wife.

As captain of the Yorkshire Red-caps, Fairfax had served against the Scots, and, like his fathers, he had won his knighthood with the sword. When Charles had called his partisans to York, he had tried to dissuade his majesty from making war; had tried by word of mouth, and by a great petition, laid with audacious hand on the royal pommel. Having urged the king in vain, he drew his sword and threw himself body and soul into the cause adopted by his father and his wife. Thirty years old, and knowing a soldier's duty, he had been appointed Master of the Yorkshire Horse. Father and son had served in a common camp; but while the father, having more fire than science, had lost as many actions as he gained, the son had marched from victory to victory. Leeds, Wetherby, Wakefield, had resounded through the land. Even his one disaster at Bradford had helped to swell the volume of his fame. Pressed on all sides, he had placed his wife in the centre of a troop, and dashed against Newcastle's lines. Whirl, flash, and stab —a hurly-burly of hoofs and voices—and he had found himself outside the lines — alone.　His troopers had been killed, and his wife had been taken prisoner; but his daring act had touched his adversary's heart, and Lady Fairfax had been sent home in Newcastle's coach, unransomed and unhurt.　New day, new fortune.　He had beaten Byron; he had crushed Bellasis; he had driven Newcastle into York; when Rupert, rushing into his field, had crowned him with the glory of Marston Moor.

That action had dispersed the cavalier forces in the north.　Rupert had retreated over Blackstone Edge.　Newcastle had gained the coast and passed the sea.　York had surrendered to the victors.

Scarred by sword, and drilled with shot, Fairfax was called to Westminster, thanked for his great service, and appointed to the chief command.

A new rule had been passed; the Self-denying Ordinance, by which members of the two Houses were forbidden to hold commissions in the field. Essex, Manchester, Denbigh, all the great peers who had opposed—and spared—the king, were pushed aside.　In theory, the captains and colonels, such as Cromwell and Waller, who had seats in the lower House, were also pushed aside; but this new rule had not yet come into force, and some of the officers were still afield. Cromwell was with Waller, in the west, hanging on the flank of Goring's horse, and holding Rupert's recruits in check ; while Fairfax was engaged with Skippon and Hugh Peters in setting up his new model on the Windsor slopes.

His first appearance showed the man. He rode to Windsor, not, like Essex, with the pomp of a great earl, attended by a train of coaches for his household, but with two or three captains of his staff. At once, the men were out, and the old companies dissolved. His army was to be a new army, ruled by a higher spirit, and with a different organic form. The companies were weeded and re-made. Bad elements were expelled ; no drunkard or poacher was allowed to stay. Swearing and thieving were forbidden ; thieving, under penalty of death. A monthly fast was ordered. Faithful and strenuous preachers were engaged ; Bowles and Sprigge, Saltmarsh and Hugh Peters. Every soldier was to attend sermons, to observe fasts, and to lead, both outwardly and inwardly, a godly life. In arm and brain the regiments were to thrill with passionate ardour. Officers of good experience and surpassing godliness were appointed to the chief commands ; Skippon, with the rank of major-general, to the foot ; Cromwell, with the rank of lieutenant-general, to the horse ; Hammond, with the rank of lieutenant-general, to the trains. Officers who had served the cause elsewhere came into Windsor ; Ireton, Montagu, Rainsborough, Deane ; all iron-fisted and fanatical men. The discipline was stern, as stern in Windsor as it was to be henceforward in the field. By drilling and parading day and night, the squads and companies were trooped and regimented, and the new model was complete :—ready to prove themselves up to their high calling—'good soldiers' and 'better saints.'

At Oxford, this modelling of a new army to replace the army lost by Essex, was regarded as a jest. 'New model ! new noddle !' laughed the courtiers, who were slow to understand how men like Fairfax and Cromwell could do what military peers like Essex and Manchester had failed to do.

The new model sprang out of Cromwell's brain. So far back as the night of Edge Hill, he had seen that riff-raff from the streets made no better fighting-men than riff-raff from the fields. Officers on the cavalier side fought better than his own. Why so ? They fought for 'honour,' and this sentiment kept their faces to the foe. To meet that pagan sentiment, he must have some Christian sentiment. He found the thing he sought in 'conscience.' Conscience, when stirred and kindled, has an awful power; a power to move the earth, and carry heaven by storm. He picked his men on a new principle. Instead of looking for brawny limbs and reckless heads, he sought for sober and God-fearing men, who loathed the devil and all his works. Light livers and loose talkers were discarded from his troop, until his regiment included none but 'saints:' men of a single hope— for which they were ready to lay down their lives. Derided by the cavaliers as fellows who made faces and sang through the nose, they taught the jesters after two or three brushes in the open to turn their wit another way: 'Lord, sirs, those boys will sing you a psalm, and then drub every one before them.' At Marston Moor, where they had ridden through Rupert's horse, as through a field of corn, they had stamped themselves the strongest regiment on the English soil.

These Ironsides were the models on which the troops at Windsor, drilling for the new campaign, were formed. The new army was a sect, burning with the ardour of an infant church.

Compared with a pacific Essex, bent on sparing Charles, and closing the unhappy feud with little or no change in church and state, Fairfax seemed a man of steel. He never dreamt of sparing Charles. He had no wish to hinder change; such things were not for him to rule. A soldier, not a politician, he regarded war as war, and on the field he thought of nothing but the end. What helped him towards that end he sought. Thus, in modelling his new army, he desired to have the author of that army by his side. Smitten by the Self-denying Ordinance, Cromwell was about to yield up his commission and retire from service in the field. Fairfax sent for him to Windsor, and at the same time he let the Houses know that Cromwell could not yet be spared. A common rule might do for common captains, but an officer like Cromwell should be treated as a man apart. Who was to face the enemy's horse? Skippon was busy with the foot, testing, forming, drilling his battalion. No man knew his business better; but the rough old soldier had never handled a troop of horse. This arm was the Lord-General's weakest arm. His infantry and his artillery were good; his cavalry was not to be compared with that of Rupert. Who could be set against the prince, except the soldier who had routed him on Marston Moor?

Cromwell arrived at Windsor. He had come up from the west, from watching Goring. He was on his way to Westminster, to give up his command and fall henceforward into private life. He came, he said. to kiss the Lord-General's hand, and take his leave. Fairfax and Cromwell were of a single mind in treating the war as war; in pushing the enemy with all their might; in leaving peace to be arranged when all the military work had first been done. Cromwell had given the word: ' If I meet the king in battle, I shall pistol him like any other man.' That was the Lord-General's plan. Next day, ere Cromwell left his room, a messenger arrived at Windsor, bringing him leave of absence from the House for forty days.

Hot work was waiting that leave. The king, who lay at Oxford, was preparing to take the field. Rupert sent out a party of horse, two thousand sabres strong, to bring his majesty, with his train and foot regiments, to the camp at Worcester. Could the intended march be stopped—the king shut up in Oxford, and the junction of the armies foiled? If any man could do the work, Cromwell was the man. Would he attempt the feat? Yea, instantly. Fairfax called out a party of horse and dragoons, such as were in the wards and about the town. They were quickly under arms. Cromwell led them out from Windsor, not staying for either money to pay them, or for stragglers to fill up their ranks.

At Islip Bridge, he struck four regiments of horse, including the Queen's Own, and routed them at a charge; capturing the queen's standard, five hundred horses, and two hundred prisoners, many of them officers and men of quality. Riding on the fugitives, who made for Blechingdon house, which Colonel Windebank held for Charles, he captured that important place of arms. Windebank was shot by Charles for giving up a fortress to a troop of horse.

Fairfax set out from Windsor, with his untried force. One day was given to prayer. Peters appealed for help to that God of Battles, who had never yet betrayed His saints. The regiments knelt in prayer: ten thousand voices swelled into the psalm. That duty done, the saints went out to seek their foe.

CHAPTER XXIII.

LAST DAYS OF ROYALTY.

1647.

Two years and two months after Fairfax marched out of Windsor, Charles appeared before the gates, attended by a troop of horse. Since quitting Windsor to begin the war, he had never ceased his hankering after the royal house. A baffled, broken man, he came again to the Upper ward, not without hope of once more gathering his family into their home under St. George's keep.

Bells were rung for him in the town, as they had rung for him in days of yore; but with a difference in the time, and therefore in the cost! Of yore, the ringers had been paid for a peal of welcome, forty pence; this time the payment was reduced to twenty-four! It was a grade on a descending scale. The king was still a king, entitled to his bells; but he was slipping from his seat, and who could say how soon his royalty might be gone? As taken by the town, the measure of his fall was two parts in five,—a fact which they recorded on the ringers' fee.

He came to Windsor under watch and ward; attended by three commissioners, and surrounded by a troop of horse. The three commissioners, Coke, Crewe, and Browne, were watching him for the lower House, now beginning to be called the Rump; the troop of horse, a part of Colonel Whalley's regiment, were guarding him for the army—now rejoicing in the name of Saints. Rump and army were at feud, and Charles was the prize and prey of these great factions in the state. The talking faction was mainly Presbyterian; the fighting faction mainly Independent. Both were in a jealous and electric mood. Charles came to Windsor in the teeth of orders from the Rump, but in connivance with officers who laughed at votes, and left him free to lodge where he pleased, so long as he kept within their lines. 'His majesty will retire to Newmarket,' the House had said; 'He is unwilling to retire,' the general had replied. Fairfax would not force the king. 'Your majesty will return to Holdenby,' urged Coke and his colleagues, speaking for the Rump. 'We have resolved to remove Ourselves to

Windsor, whither We have sent on part of Our stuff already,' answered Charles, in his most kingly style. 'On Thursday, We shall set out towards that place.' Coke produced his orders from the House. Charles simply added: 'After we have come to Windsor, if you move Us further, you shall have Our answer.' Whalley stood aloof, having no orders from his general. In the teeth of Coke, the king set out, safe in the protection of Whalley's troop.

Whichcot received the royal visitor. When Fairfax marched from Windsor, Venn had been called to other work,—to beating up new saints, and drilling them into companies. Tossing off his beaker at the White Hart, with mayor and aldermen, he had gallopped off, leaving in town and keep the memory of a hearty soldier and a godly man. Not yet was Charles to meet his old tormentor from the city face to face. Whichcot, a neutral colonel, with some love of art, and yet open to the witcheries of sack and sugar, had been voted governor in his stead. Rainsborough was left at Windsor with his regiment, holding the town and bridge, as part of the Lord-General's lines. The Castle was a separate post, depending on a public vote. So far as the two factions were concerned, Whichcot was a servant of the Rump.

This man received his majesty from Whalley's troop, and, once within the gates, he took command of the royal guard.

In outward seeming, Charles was free. He gave his orders, and those orders were obeyed. All caps were doffed to him, all knees were bent to him, as in the olden time. It was a privilege to kiss his hand. No one addressed him otherwise than as his majesty. The Castle was regarded as his house ; no one opposed his lodging in the Tudor tower. The gallery, the guard-room, staircase, with their wealth of art and furniture, were his own. Two of his favourite chaplains, three of his favourite bedchamber-men, were at his side. Some people fancied he had come for good. Such, also, was the royal hope :—one more illusion of that dreamy, plastic, and poetic brain.

Great things had happened since the day when Fairfax marched from Windsor with his twenty thousand saints. England had been subdued. Not only had the king and cavaliers been crushed, but parliament and people had been overborne. Never, since the days of Lion Heart, had such English troops been hurled against a foe. No passion save religious zeal—the fervour of a crusade, or the fury of an infant church—has ever lent such strength, has ever lit such fire, as strained and glowed within those Windsor columns. Once in motion, nothing had been able to arrest their march. When they set out, the king was master of the west and midlands. In the western counties, only Plymouth and Taunton stood against him; Wilts was his, with the exception of a single town; Dorset and Hants were his, with the exception of four or five ports, protected by the fleet; Oxford-shire was his, with the one exception of Henley Bridge. In Berks he held Wallingford, Farring-don, and Radcot Bridge. Master of his move-ments, he was free to advance towards either York or Westminster, while his opponents were compelled to cover London, where the Houses sat, and at the same time succour Taunton, where Blake was stewing his last pair of boots. His majesty's force out-numbered the new model many times; yet, in less than twelve months from that going out of Windsor, all his armies had been shivered, all his cities taken, all his strongholds stormed.

Naseby had announced the new model. Less than eight thousand saints had cut down, captured, or dispersed a royal army, led by Rupert, Maurice, and the king. Charles had fallen back on Oxford, never to make head again. Rupert and Maurice had retired into the west to make one futile effort more, and then to fly beyond the seas. Driving the fugitives along, the saints had entered Leicester and Highworth, relieved the garrison of Taunton, beaten their foes at Ilmore and Lamport, stormed B idgewater, occupied Bath, stormed Bristol, taken Devizes and Laycock house, stormed Barclay and Tiverton castles, broken into Cornwall, captured Goring's horse, reduced the whole west country, forcing Hopton's army to surrender and disband, and then advanced towards Oxford, whence the king, unwilling to be taken, had escaped into the north. Masters of Oxford, the Ironsides were masters of the realm.

Disguised as a groom, the king had thrown himself on his native Scots. His native Scots had treated him no better than the southern saints. Finding him fretful and morose,—apt to call names, as 'rebel' and 'schismatic,' and to describe their covenant as a 'damned covenant,' and their country as a wretched place, to which nothing on earth would make him go,—they had set their teeth against him, and had sold him to the Rump. At

Holdenby, he had learnt, to his great joy, that the talking men and the fighting men were falling out; and each, in passion with the other, bidding for the king's support. A prisoner of the Rump, bought with their money, he had welcomed the visit of Cornet Joyce, the tailor, who had carried him to head-quarters. There, he had been well received. Fairfax had kissed his hand; and some of the officers were supposed to have said, that if he joined them against the Rump, they would set him on his throne again. Whalley, appointed by Fairfax to command his guard, had been less severe than Coke; and Charles had taken his cue from Whalley rather than from the Rump commissioner. Thus he had arrived at Windsor in defiance of the Rump.

But Charles at Windsor was no nearer to his ends; the gathering of his children and the settlement of his household under a common roof. His family were scattered far and wide. The queen and Prince of Wales were at St. Germains; Mary of Orange, his eldest daughter, was at the Hague. James, duke of York, Henry, the boy duke of Gloucester, and Elizabeth, their sister, were at St. James's palace. Henriette, whom he had never seen, was with her nurse in France. When he was carried off by Joyce, the three children still in England were at Hampton Court; but they had been withdrawn, lest they should also fall into the power of some other Cornet Joyce. He asked to have his children come to him at Windsor, and the House refused. The Prince of Wales being gone, James, duke of York, stood next in order to the throne. He could be played against the king. More than one plot had been formed to steal him. Northumberland, his guardian, had declined to answer for his safety, since these plots were formed with the duke's assent. To let him pass within the military lines, even on the pretence of seeing his father, was to give him up to Fairfax and the saints. Neither Lords nor Commons would consent to such an act.

Nor was he luckier with his household. Hammond and Sheldon, his domestic chaplains, were obnoxious to the Rump. William Hammond, doctor of divinity, had been public orator in Oxford, prebendary of Christchurch, archdeacon of Chichester, and the king's commissioner for his church affairs. After the king's retreat from Oxford, he had been put out of his livings by the Rump, and had not seen his majesty again till his removal to Windsor. Here he had joined him, but against the will of Coke. Murray, Kirk, and Leveston, the three bedchamber-men, were hardly less obnoxious to the Rump. Coke protested against their presence, and demanded their exclusion from the royal house. Charles turned aside. Fairfax spoke so softly that he felt secure of his support. He failed to see that Whichcot was in charge, and must obey his masters of the Rump. Whichcot was no fanatic. Since his coming to Windsor, he had done his best to save what might be saved, and to restore what might be found among the wreck. To him, St. George's chapel was a shrine. He mourned in spirit over the despoiler's work. He sought to gather up the wreckage and replace the stalls and ornaments in the choir. But he was not an English-papist, and he never flinched from doing his duty to the state. When ordered by Coke to clear the Castle of Hammond and the rest, he instantly obeyed.

The king entreated Fairfax to protect his servants, and to let him see his children. Fairfax answered him, that if his majesty joined head-quarters, something might be done. Neither Fairfax nor Cromwell cared whether Hammond were with the king or not ; and they were both content that he should see his children when and where he liked. But they could hardly use their force. Windsor was in Whichcot's hands. To interfere with his command was war, and they were not prepared to start a second civil war. A middle course was tried. Head-quarters were removed to Reading, and his majesty was offered Lord Craven's house in Caversham park. There, he might have his chaplains and see his children, under the protection of an Ironside guard.

Charles clung with great tenacity to his house; but in that house he was no longer free. At Craven's house he would be more at large, and nearer to the source of power. So he set out again; his hopes all lying in the victor's camp.

CHAPTER XXIV.

SAINTS IN COUNCIL.

1647.

HARDLY was the king gone from Windsor, when Fairfax moved some troops into the keep—as an experiment. Only a hundred came; but they were placed under chosen officers, free from the control of Whichcot and the Rump. 'Provide the money for these men,' he wrote to Lenthall; 'the garrison being too weak, the Castle too important' to be left alone. At first the house stood out; but Fairfax threw fresh troops into the keep and town; and Whichcot, though not displaced as governor, found himself gently pushed aside. Armed men are not expected to lie down and starve. The saints were fond of Scripture, and their favourite quotation was: 'The earth is the Lord's;' to which they added, 'and the fruits thereof are His saints.' The ordinary garrison was in arrear of pay ; no less than twelve months in arrear ; yet, after some delays, the House saw fit to pay the Lord-General's men.

A few weeks later, Fairfax moved his army into Windsor, and established his head-quarters in the royal house. Respect for Charles had so far held him back ; but now all feeling of respect was gone ; forfeited by what he held to be an extra-ordinary breach of faith. From first to last, he had treated the king with courtesy ; at times with more than courtesy. At Caversham park, he had allowed him to have his chaplain and to see his children. To procure him the gratification of seeing his children, had not been an easy task. Parliament was jealous ; fearing the dangers of the road, the chance of rescue, and the likelihood that Charles might try to keep them. Fairfax had pledged his faith for Charles. At Hampton Court, to which the king had moved from Caversham, on account of plague, he had permitted the soft-spoken Whalley to attend him, and command his guard. Yet, contrary to his honourable understanding, Charles had stolen away from Hampton court, and flung himself into the Isle of Wight. All ties were severed by that breach of faith. Marching into Windsor, Fairfax unfurled his banner on the royal hill. With Charles, the Stuart flag went down; and now, the old red cross—the cross of Cressy, Sluys, and Agincourt—streamed, as in Elizabeth's period, from the flag-staff on St. George's keep.

A council met. Letters had come from the Isle of Wight; letters from the governor, Colonel Hammond, with a case of conscience; in the language of the sect, a case of 'temptation.' Hammond had the king thrown suddenly on his hands. In a divided duty, he was 'tempted' on many sides. He wished the officers at Windsor to understand the facts. Could they assist him to see his way?

Robert Hammond, the 'dear Robin' of Cromwell's letters, was a nephew of Henry Hammond, the court chaplain; also a nephew of Thomas Hammond, the lieutenant - general of artillery. Thus he had an uncle on either side. In politics he stood between these two extremes. Less courtly than his uncle, the chaplain, he was also less sectarian than his uncle, the lieutenant-general. Flighty enough to have fought a duel and killed his man, he was serious enough to have served under Essex and to have suffered captivity in Basing house. Early in life he had married a daughter of John Hampden, and had learned his politics from his sober, and yet moderate, father-in-law. By that alliance, he had come into the cousinry of Cromwell; but he had never been able to go that cousin's lengths. Like a major part of his countrymen, he was for king and parliament; hoping for a speedy and solid peace, on terms that should leave the king royal, and the nation free.

Some weeks ago, this officer had called at Hampton Court to see his uncle, the chaplain, who had introduced him to his majesty. Charles had posed before 'dear Robin,' as he had done before Falkland. Dazzled by royal flatteries, Robin had been loose of tongue, and, in his warmth of words, had brewed strange fancies in the dreamer's brain. Charles had followed him to the Isle of Wight, and, taking him in the moment of surprise, had got from him a promise to defend his freedom and his life. Afterwards, Robin had bethought him of his civic duty, of his military oath. He was a servant of the House. Charles was a property of that House, no less than a fugitive from head-quarters. Parliament might demand him, and head-quarters might demand him. Which authority should he obey? Could he, in honour, give the king up to either? Charles was his guest, living under his roof, in the protection of his solemn pledge. This was Robin's temptation. How was a soldier, wanting to do right, to take three opposite ways?

Steel-clad, inflexible Cromwell, snatching a pen, despatched from Windsor ten or twelve lines which opened poor Robin's eyes. There was no room for doubt. Charles Stuart was a fugitive from the army, and must be held in trust until the army had decided on his fate.

The council met again. 'What shall now be done with the king?' This question was debated day and night; by ministers in the camp, by troopers in the ale-house yards, by general officers in the Keep. Saints, male and female, flocked to Windsor, bearing messages from above, made known to them in dreams and visions of the night. These visitors, pale and haggard in appearance, cooed like doves and shrieked like ravens. Fasting hard and preaching fervently, they sometimes fell, from sheer exhaustion, into fits, in which they jerked, and foamed, and seemed to be possessed. One of these saints was Saltmarsh, chaplain of the army, and a favourite of the Saints. Born in Yorkshire, educated at Cambridge, he had passed through the ministry from Northampton to Braisted,

and from Braisted to Ilford. Gifted with some
fancy, he had written prose and verse ; but his
strength was in the pulpit, not the pen. Like Peters,
he could rouse and madden the excited troops.
For Fairfax he professed a reverence bordering on
idolatry ; but he was always free with his advice,
convinced that he was guided by the Holy Spirit.
The soldiers liked him, and the officers feared him
—as a man above the articles of war. Sinners in
high places trembled at his voice. Sinners in low
places died beneath his frown. These saints were
ten times more fanatical than Cromwell or Ireton,
fifty times more presumptuous than Laud or Wren.
They claimed to rule the rulers, and to wrest the
sword from the victor's hand. They preached by
day and night, but not one word of either chivalry
or charity fell from their lips in town and camp.

Cromwell, Ireton, and their colleagues met again.
Cromwell prayed for light, and, in his vehement
words, he seemed to strike out light as with the
flashing of his sword. Inspired by him, men
suddenly saw their way, or fancied that they saw
their way. On empty stomachs and on much
debate these general officers resolved, that Charles
Stuart should be put on trial as a public criminal.

Hereon the male and female saints dispersed.

One, at least, of the Council let the king understand privately, that, though he voted with the rest, his heart was not in the vote. Saltmarsh went home to Ilford, where he told his wife the wonders he had seen. Yet many of the elder race of saints were discontented and morose. Some wanted to put down Charles, and set up Christ. Some wished to abolish peers, councillors, and civil magistrates, as useless lumber in a kingdom of the saints. Others declared against captains, colonels, and general officers. Those who had not joined the new model, protested that the Ironsides were not the only saints, though God had given them a share of victory. Cromwell spoke of the Ironsides as the army, and pretended that a man was not a soldier unless enrolled under the Windsor flag. Lilburne, and others, who had never served in the new model, rose against these pretensions. Windsor, he said, was not the only Zion, and he raised the standard of revolt at Ware.

Fairfax had rough work on hand. But Cromwell, taking some troops of horse from Windsor, rode on the men of Ware, broke up the rival camp, and brought the protesting saints to Windsor, where the leaders were put in ward, and tried by court-martial for the crime of mutiny.

On Friday, December 3rd, a corporal was condemned to death, and six soldiers were condemned to run the gauntlet on the following day.

That night, as Saltmarsh lay in bed, a vision came to him. He was commanded to get up, take horse, go forth to Windsor, and rebuke the generals for their dealings with the saints. Springing from his bed, he told his wife that he must instantly be gone to Windsor, having something to reveal from Heaven, which it behoved his comrades of the army to understand. He made his way to London ; it was Saturday night when he arrived ; too late to seek a horse and take the road. Next morning, he set out. The days were short, and in the darkness he lost his way ; wandering up and down the lanes and heaths all night. On Monday he crossed the bridge, and called some officers who were out on duty to his side, to tell them he had come back in the name of Heaven to warn them against their evil deeds, and to announce a day of wrath. Knowing him well, these officers listened to the old minister's words with awe. He then walked up to the Castle, where the Council was about to meet. He walked into the room and bade them listen to his voice. In other times, he said, he had come to them in the spirit of a lamb; now he had returned to them in the spirit of a lion. In a trance, the Lord had made Himself known to him, and had sent him to declare His will. Aforetime, He had done much for them, and much by them; but now He had forsaken them because they had forsaken Him. They had forgotten their first principle; they had persecuted and imprisoned His saints. He would no longer prosper their councils, but would divide them and destroy them; because they had attempted to destroy the people of God. Leaving the council, he repaired to the Lord-General, and on entering his presence, refused to doff his hat. Stern of voice and sad of aspect, he told the general he had formerly doted on his person so much as to give offence to God. Now he had no command to honour him at all. God, he had come to say, was highly displeased with him, and would no longer prosper him. From Fairfax he went to Cromwell, and required him in the name of Heaven to set the soldiers whom he had taken, free. Again, he wore his hat. Next day, he took his leave, telling the officers that he had done his errand as commanded from above. His work on earth was over; he should see his friends no more. Five days afterwards, they heard that he had gone to London, where he had taken leave of friends, telling them his work was done, and asking them to sustain his wife, and then gone home, laid down, and died.

CHAPTER XXV.

CHANGING SIDES.

1648.

Events and purposes changed from day to day, and every change in either camp or court, threw people into new relations to the cause. Less by their own movements of opinion than by the march of events, men who had been fighting on one side, found themselves not unfrequently ranged on the other side. Roundheads passed over to the court; and cavaliers rode over to the camp. Each had to bear the consequence of his change of front.

In the strong-room of the Norman tower, this record of a former tenant meets the eye:

Brown Bushel.

/48.

Brown Bushel was a sea-captain. At the outset, he had gone with his ship and with his fleet under Pennington, for the king. Afterwards, under the earl of Warwick, he had gone for king and parliament. Like other sailors, he knew little of politics, but he had that feeling of the sea which leads a sailor to stand by his admiral and his ship. An excellent seaman, prompt and steady, he had done the state good service. Twice he had been thanked by the House of Commons; once for an act of gallantry in seizing the frigate *Maria;* a second time for his alertness in landing at the port, and capturing the castle of Scarborough. Like other captains, he had afterwards passed over to the king, he and his ship and crew; not of his own free will, so much as by the accidents of time and place. On Charles being taken prisoner, he had returned to England, thinking the war was over, and expecting to live unnoticed in the crowd. He held the General's pass, and was unconscious of having put his life in jeopardy; but he was closely watched, and more than once he had been summoned to appear, and answer for himself. As time wore on, he had felt himself more safe. Then had come a critical time. No less than seventeen ships of war renounced their flag, submitted to the king, and talked of visiting the Isle of Wight.

Sailors of Bushel's stamp were not to be safely left at large. One day he was arrested in his lodgings, charged with usual 'acts of piracy,' and committed to the Norman tower. Here he inscribed this record of his name and date.

A court-martial, sitting at Windsor, and composed of soldiers, not sailors, sentenced him to death; but he was left in jail, apparently overlooked, for the next three years. Not until Rupert 'turned pirate' was Bushel's offence remembered, and the sentence of his judges carried out. Taken to Tower hill, he had the strange fate of suffering at the same time and on the same scaffold with Christopher Love, pastor of St. Lawrence Jewry, one of the most powerful gospellers of the civil war.

Not far from that record of a gallant but unlucky mariner, appears this record of a not less gallant and unlucky soldier:

R.   L.

Below these letters hangs a shield; the arms of Rowland Langhorne, once a major-general in the roundhead army, and the hero of Shrewsbury, Haverford-west, and many other fights.

Near to this inscription by Rowland Langhorne may be seen a second and a third inscription:

SIR HARRY STRADLING.

I. STRADLING.

Under each of these two names hangs a shield; the family coat-of-arms.

The two Stradlings, uncle and nephew, were officers in the royalist army, and their lines were woven in and out with those of Rowland Langhorne; closer, in truth, both in their lives and deaths than these records, cut with their own knives in the Norman tower.

Reared in the household of Lord Essex, whom he had served from a page upwards, Langhorne went with his master to the Netherlands, where he had studied with assiduity the trade of war. A western man, with manors and connexions in the border counties, he had proved extremely useful to the cause of which his master was the military chief. First as captain, afterwards as colonel, he had striven against the cavaliers, and kept a party for the parliament in what were thought to be exclusively royalist shires. One striking action—his surprise of Shrewsbury—broke up the negotiations at Uxbridge, one of the most striking features of the war.

Shrewsbury, the strongest fortress in the border country, was the royalist capital of the west, as Oxford was the royalist capital in the midlands. There, the king had kept his court; there, Rupert had a permanent camp; the district round the Wrekin being his principal recruiting ground. Shrewsbury connected Chester with Chepstow, in a line which covered the mountainous countries on the west. That Shrewsbury lay exposed to danger was so little dreamt, that most of the gentry serving in the field had sent their wives and children, their plate and money, to the town. Like other places, Shrewsbury was divided in opinion; the gentry going mostly for the king, the burghers going mostly for the king and parliament. On this division, Langhorne had laid his plans. Scouts had crept into the town, where they beat up friends, and mixed among the troops. Sir Michael Earnly, governor of the town, a soldier of repute, was sick; unable, they had found, to leave his bed. The staff was careless, and the men, expecting no attack, were off their guard. Still the garrison was strong, and, if alarmed in time, was likely to make a good defence. Langhorne had tried a ruse. By sending to the town a tale of enemies being seen at such and such places, he had caused the best and readiest of the troops to be marched beyond striking distance of the town. Some burghers had agreed to open one of their gates, and lend such help as burghers can afford in a nocturnal fight. Creeping under cover of darkness to the city wall, Langhorne had entered by that open gate, rushed through the streets, occupied the market-place, and broken into the citadel. Starting at the first alarm, Earnly had risen from his sick bed, and run out in his shirt. A roundhead trooper raised his gun, and asked him whether he demanded quarter. 'Never!' cried the old soldier, and was instantly shot down. At daybreak, Shrewsbury was in Langhorne's power, with all the cavaliers' wives and children, plate and money. Eight knights and baronets, forty captains and colonels, with two hundred horsemen, were his prize of war.

Next year, having risen from the rank of colonel to that of major-general, he had fought at Haverford-west, where he had first crossed swords with the Stradlings, afterwards to be his comrades in the Norman tower.

Among the prisoners taken on the field at Edge Hill, was Colonel Sir Edward Stradling, chief of the Welsh family of St. Donats' in Glamorgan, a man who boasted of being the first baronet in Wales. The house was royalist. Long before blood was drawn, Sir Edward had been summoned to Westminster as a delinquent. His reply had been, to raise his county for the king, to leave John, his second son, the task of keeping order, and to join the royal army with his tenants. Fighting by the side of Lunsford, he had been taken, like that one-eyed monster, and disarmed.

Sir Harry, his brother, had been at sea, captain of the *Bonaventure*, serving on the Irish coast, when Warwick had seized the fleet. Sir Harry, royalist to the bone, had tried to save his ship, but his own men had put him under guard, and kept him prisoner in his ship till they could land him at the nearest port. Landing in Wales, he had made his way to his nephew's camp, where he had proved a useful ally in defending creeks and river mouths against the roundhead fleet.

John Stradling, better soldier than his father, had risen from captain to colonel, from colonel to major-general; rising with the enemy he had now to fight. A corner of the island, torn by the waters into inlets, bays, and havens, Pembrokeshire was easy to attack by sea, but very difficult to approach by land. None but a local man, with large connexions, could invade so strong a shire. Langhorne crossed the hills, his deed at Shrewsbury going before him like a blast. Pembroke and Haverford-west were strongly held. Stradling lay in the county town, and Langhorne turned his face that way. A charge, delivered some days after Naseby, ended in a clear victory. Stradling fell back, the county town surrendered, and the hope of finding an asylum in South Wales was gone.

Langhorne was created general of four counties of Wales. A house was settled on his wife. Guns, men, and money, were supplied, that he might follow up his victory and complete his task by the conquest and occupation of Pembroke, arsenal, port, and town. Driving his enemies from post to post, he had cooped them up in Pembroke, where Colonel Poyer held the chief command. But neither gates nor guns had been able to stay his march. Crushing through all obstacles, he had broken into the place, and taken the defenders captive; Poyer, Powel, and the two Stradlings, being amongst his prize.

His work was done, his party served. Hero of a day and a debate, he was rewarded by the House of Commons with a rich delinquent's lands. From Dee to Severn, the whole of Wales was placed under his control. Yet, on the heels of his success had followed the gravest doubts. Was he doing right in strengthening the men at Windsor, who were building up so vast a military power? Like his old master, he had always fought for peace. When Charles was taken, he had been sorely exercised in spirit. That was not the end for which he had drawn his sword. To preserve the king and kingdom, not to upset them for the benefit of a sect, had been his constant aim. When he found time to think, Poyer and the Stradlings seemed to him better patriots than Cromwell. In his conversations with his prisoners, he was gradually drawn over to their views, and, being satisfied that his old courses had been wrong, he offered to undo his work. Charles gladly promised him his pardon and support. But all such secrets were betrayed, and Langhorne was required by parliament to report himself in the Irish camp. Should any of his men refuse to cross the sea, he was to break them up and send them home. Disgusted by this order, he dismantled Tenby, carried off the guns and stores, and ran up the royal flag at Pembroke, having no fear of the offended saints.

Yet, in a few weeks, he and his new friends were at Windsor. Cromwell had rushed on Pembroke, borrowed guns from a war-ship, stormed and starved the town into surrender. Certain persons were excepted from the terms: Langhorne, Poyer, and Powel, and some others; men who had sinned more than the royalists, in having 'fought against the light.'

Stradling died in the Norman tower.

Tried by court-martial, Langhorne, Poyer, and Powel, were sentenced to be shot. Fairfax reduced the sentence to a single death, and ordered them to select the one who was to die, by lot.

'Life given by God,' was written on slips of paper. One of the slips was left a blank. A child was asked to draw the slips. The blank was given to Poyer, who was taken out and shot.

The name and date:

R. POWEL.

/48.

are visible on the prison wall, with a depending shield, like that of Stradling, that of Langhorne.

Langhorne's fate was tragic. Released from custody, he crossed to Ireland, with a lowered rank ; went over to the king once more, was taken prisoner, tried for desertion, and shot to death.

CHAPTER XXVI.

BAGSHOT LODGE.

1648.

TIME : *Saturday, December twenty-second.*

Route : Farnham to Bagshot Lodge, twelve miles, more or less ; Bagshot Lodge to Windsor Castle, ten miles, more or less.   At Bagshot Lodge, halt for two hours.

Ten troops of horse moved out of Farnham, on the road through Aldershot towards the royal lodge ; two thousand casques and sword-points gleaming round the king ; a prisoner on his way from a dungeon in Hurst Castle, to the military head-quarters at Windsor.   Harrison, the Anabaptist gospeller and major-general, rode at the king's side in his black casque and armour, grim and silent as a man of stone.   The march was slow ; at almost every rut or rise the king's horse plunged or dropped.   The beast grew lame ; and every one got fagged, and out of sorts. At Bagshot Lodge, they cried a halt.

On slipping from his saddle at the gate, his majesty remarked to Harrison, that his brute was nought, and that he must change him for a better mount. His tenants at the lodge, he said, bred horses, and could easily find him a beast that he could ride. The Anabaptist heard, but held his tongue. A rider, spending his life on horseback, he had seen enough. The horse was not at fault; but he pretended not to see the trick. His duty was to act, and not to prate.

Bagshot Lodge was in the royal forest, and was held by license from the crown. The tenants, Lord and Lady Newburgh, knelt to receive the king as he got down. Charles raised them in his arms. To kneel to him was a forbidden courtesy. He was no longer recognised as king, or spoken to as king. His name was Stuart; Charles Stuart; nothing more. Harrison, indeed, uncapped when speaking, but the Anabaptist spoke but seldom; and his officers seemed to have forgotten every-thing about his majesty's ' sacred rights.' Lady Newburgh led the king in. To his amazement, stair and corridor, closet and dining-room, were lined with troops ; dark, speechless men, clad in black casques and breast-plates, and carrying naked swords. No privacy was to be expected there.

Bagshot Lodge was a suspected place, at which the Anabaptist major-general had not readily agreed to halt. When Charles had first named the place he had demurred. Why so ? Bagshot was on the way to Windsor, and a sort of half-way house. His orders were understood to leave the king free on minor points—his pace in riding, and his choice of halting ground — so far as could be safely ventured. On the other hand, attempts at flight, if not at rescue, were to be expected on the road. Now Lord and Lady Newburgh were not only the king's tenants, but were known to have had their part in many a desperate plot. Their house might prove a snare.

Yet, looking at his troops, the heroes of a hundred battle-fields, he had nodded his assent. On drawing near the forest, he had pushed a squadron forward to invest the lodge, search all the offices and rooms, and scour the rides and coverts of adjacent woods. So far, the game was running on all-fours. Charles was at Bagshot Lodge ; his horse was lamed ; but Harrison's suspicions were excited, and his officers were on their guard. Stair, corridor, and room, were held by silent, listening men. No private speech with either host or hostess was allowed. If Charles were free to dine and chat, his dining and his chatting must be done in presence and in hearing of his guards.

Charles was at bay; a prisoner, as he felt convinced, to enemies who were hurrying him on to trial, sentence, and the block. He knew those enemies well; he had not shown them mercy, and he had no mercy to expect from them. Few of his friends were left; Holland, Hamilton, Capel, Goring, Loughborough, all had failed. Most of these peers were prisoners in St. George's keep. Ashburnham and Legge, his personal servants, shared their prison. Windsor had become the dungeon and the tomb of his adherents. Force had failed; the sword lay broken in his hand. What then was left? His wit, his courage; if he had wit or courage left; his wit and courage, aided by some accidents of time and place.

Here, briefly noted, were his hopes—which he imagined were his plans.

Sitting at the board, and hanging by the couch, he was to linger at the lodge as long as Harrison's patience could be taxed. On starting, he was to mount a very swift horse, slip through his guard, and dart into the thicket, in and out of which no stranger to the forest would be able to keep his pace. He was a perfect master of his horse. Few riders held so light a rein, and made the beast he rode so much a portion of himself. Once clear of his pursuers, he had little need to fear. In every corner of the chase he was at home; and more than all, he knew the district lying between the Castle and the lodge. In other days, these regions had been his hunting-grounds. Times without number he had cantered to the lodge—rested and dined —and cantered back at night by Swinley rayles, Inglemore pond, and Cranborne chase. No pupil of Aminadab threaded bush and brake, and followed game to their scent cover, with a nimbler foot than he. Clough, dell, and cabin, were familiar to his eye. Once free from his guard, he had a chance of hiding in the woods for days and weeks; time long enough for his servants to provide him with the means of getting to the coast and crossing over into France.

Everything, he supposed, was ready at the lodge. Lord and Lady Newburgh were devoted to his person and his cause; the lord to his person and the lady to his cause. Knowing them well, he loved them, and trusted them with all his heart. Newburgh, like himself, was fond of horses, and his stud in Bagshot park was famous on every racecourse and in every hunting-field. One of his horses was unmatched for strength and speed; nothing on four legs being able to go so fast and stay so long. That hunter was to save the king. Newburgh, faithful and fearless, was a man to run all risks, and lay his life down joyfully for his prince.

Kate, his wife, while no less brave and loyal, had the advantage of a keener wit and a more fertile brain. Kate was a catholic, and her devotion to the king was part of her devotion to the church. It was her passion to have suffered in his cause. Aubigny, her first husband, had been slain at Edge Hill; but Kate, instead of moping by his grave, had flung herself into the lines of strife. Charles had much need of female help, and Kate turned out a schemer of the foremost rank. Seeking the post of danger, she had stolen into Westminster, where she had lived and laboured as a spy, a go-between, a royalist agent. Compromised in the Waller plot, she had been arrested, and was likely to have lost her head; but she had slipt her jailer, crossed the military lines, and got into Oxford, where the royalists were in strength. So long as hope was left, she had kept the field, and when the sword was put away, she had asked for other work. To serve the king, she had married Newburgh, settled in the forest, and assisted in the stud. No less intimate with the queen than with the king, she kept the royal cyphers, and the letters passing between the royal pair flowed mostly through her pen. She knew of the intended flight, and was the chief contriver of his plan.

The lady had bad news for Charles. It was not easy to converse, in presence of these men on duty, but she managed to let him know that her swiftest hunter had been injured by a kick. His stable mate had lunged at him, so that he was unable to leave his stall. The king's heart fell. The hunter lamed ! Yes, lamed ; but she contrived to hint that she had other horses very near as good, and several that were good enough for his attempt. Charles shrank from her brave words ; though he kept up his pose and smile, in presence of his guard.

Time up, the troopers mounted. Harrison signalled to the king ; but Charles was not yet ready to proceed. An hour dragged on ; the day began to wane. Kate found the means of telling him that the other details of his scheme held good. Four or five grooms, with horses ready saddled, were in certain stations in the forest, should he need the help of either man or beast. Newburgh would ride with him, and turn all chances of the road to good account. But she was trying to kindle stone. Charles mused and mused; unable to fix his mind. Again the Anabaptist came. Time had been up long ago. Charles begged a little more time; saying he would show them a shorter cut to Windsor than the public road.

When he stept out, he found a horse at the door; a trooper's horse, instead of Lady Newburgh's choice. Harrison beckoned him to mount. The king's heart failed him more and more. His farewell to his hostess told her, she would hear his voice no more.

Rain fell heavily, as they took the path and headed through the woods. Newburgh rode out a little way, but he was soon turned back. No chance of flight occurred. A hundred men—picked riders, certain shots—rode outward, in the front and on the flanks, with pistols primed and cocked. The ranks closed up. To slip that leash —to face that ring of fire—was death. The horse rode forward in the rain, through ruts and pools, and under dripping oaks. Their shorter cut took longer time. To them, it was the old, old story:

—in the smaller things as in the greater, no one could depend on Charles. His science was to lie with truth. ' A short way, not a fair !' Men soaked with rain, and foul with mire, were in no mood to laugh at such royal jokes.

Newburgh slunk home to Bagshot park, convinced that his master's chance of breaking from his enemy was gone.

CHAPTER XXVII.

AT LENGTH.

1648–9.

Crowds filled the market-place, and poured along the Bagshot road, as the brigade of horse rode into Windsor. Never before had such a sight been seen. The king a prisoner, taken in a time of peace, and brought in as a culprit to the royal house! The crowd was deeply touched. Men who had not loved their sovereign, looked on that spectacle with dismay. Few of those burgesses had dreamt of going so far. A sense of pity and of pain sprung up in many hearts as he was swept along in that ominous cloud of horse. Some voices sobbed, 'God bless him!' Was the stream of sympathy about to turn? 'Long may he reign!' was heard in High Street. But the sentiment was confined to sobs and cries. New masters ruled the land. All Windsor was aware that only two days ago, the mayor and men of Winchester, on daring to approach the king, had been trampled in the mire by those troops of horse. No one in Windsor wanted to be kicked and pounded under stallions' hoofs; but this repression of the public voice brought up the question :—what had England gained by putting down a feudal prince, and setting up a military sect?

Burgesses who asked this question, had not long to wait for their reply.

Though Charles passed in, and all the Castle gates were closed, a crowd still lingered in the street, and strayed into the taverns, busy with the day's events. Some spoke for Charles, because the man was down. Some drank his health, with 'three times three.' The guards turned out, and cleared the street. Flying before the firelocks, people pushed into the yards and taverns. One tavern door was locked and barred against the troops, who broke the panels and discharged their pieces on the crowd. Three of the burgesses fell dead. The rest were marched to prison, and left there in the winter cold, till a court-martial should have time to punish them under military rule.

Thirty-nine days elapsed between their slaughter

at his Castle-gate and the king's execution in front of his palace at Whitehall. During those thirty-nine days, his conduct was so fine as to distract the whole country with regret that such a man should have fallen from the throne. His words were mild, his manners gracious. He exhibited no malice and no petulance. He was constant in his faith. Asking for law, he asked for nothing but the law. In patience, tenderness, and charity, he had the bearing of a saint.

On reaching the guard-room, he and his jailers were received by Whichcot, governor of the Castle, who informed him that, having been deposed by the army, he was no longer to be lodged in the royal house. A corner of the edifice had been assigned to him, and within that corner he might pick and choose. He smiled, as though such things were trifles, like the rain and slush. They thought him in a 'merry' mood, not guessing at the agonies in his breast. Walking to the corner, where he was allowed to lodge, he chose the rooms in which he wished to dine and sleep. They were unfit for use, but Whichcot called in men, who made them ready for the night. No murmur came from Charles. When told that, being deposed, he was not to be served on the knee, he answered, that such service was a thing indifferent, never exacted by a prince, but left to every man's sense of what was fit. His officers were free to either kneel or not to kneel. At supper, having no chaplain near, he took the desk, read out the lesson, offered up a prayer, and expounded the sacred text. This was a habit of his life; and he performed it well. The saints were much impressed. At length, they quitted him for the night, but ere they went away, they turned the keys and shot the bolts and bars.

The holy season being nigh, he begged to have the service of his chaplain, Dr. Hammond, whom the governor had formerly expelled. This consolation was refused. He mentioned other chaplains, but his prayer was put aside. His jailers set no store on holy seasons, calling them papistry and idolatry. Holy season or unholy season, he should have no more of his papistry at Windsor; neither should he have a chance of forming a plot, and making fresh attempts to fly. Orders from head-quarters forbade him to speak with any one in private, unless they came to him under special warrant from the general or the House. To ease the rigour of his restraint, he pledged his word to Whichcot that he would not steal away, nor seek his liberty except by honourable means. Yet he was shut in his room, kept behind locks and bars, with sentries at his door by night and day. He craved permission to write to the queen, his wife, and to the prince, his son. These graces were denied.

Some of his janitors told him that the troops insisted on his trial, as a criminal, and that a court had been appointed, chiefly of their officers, to try him for his life. Cromwell was on the list; Fairfax on the list; Venn, Whalley, Ireton, Ludlow, were on the list.

'In what way can they do it?' asked the king.

The troops accused him, he was told, of having trampled on the laws, of having caused the death of a hundred thousand men, with all the misery of a seven years' war, by separating from his parliament, and setting up his standard in defence of arbitrary and illegal power. By these offences he had forfeited his trust.

'How can they frame a charge?' he asked. Here lay his strength. There was no law by which he could be tried. A legend had been lately framed — a legend setting forth, that 'under God, the people is the source of power;' but this new principle was a phrase, and nothing more. It had no force of law, for it had never been adopted and enrolled. No article in the statute-book allowed a soldier, or a camp of soldiers, to accuse the king. How could they frame a charge?

Turning his point, they assured him that nothing of the kind was to be done; but since the question had been raised, they asked him what he would do if he were charged, like any other man, according to the law? The query was a trap; but he was frank and open. 'If they should charge me, I will make no answer; if they put me to death, I shall die like a martyr, patiently.'

On Friday, January 19th, he was taken from Windsor by the Anabaptist and his black horse. On February 7th he was brought back—dead. Tried by the sword, which he had first invoked, he had now fallen by the sword. But his trial was an act of war. Law there was none. He was indicted in the name of ' the English people ;' but the veil of sophistry had been torn aside. ' No,' cried a lady in the gallery; ' not a hundredth part of them.' The voice was that of Lady Fairfax, the Lord-General's wife. A Puritan in creed, Lady Fairfax had been a partner in her husband's toils ; but she was conscious that the king was called to answer, not before the English people, but a court of officers. So she had traversed the fiction: 'not a hundredth part of them.' Neither she nor the Lord-General sat in that court a second time.

Five hundred pounds were voted for the funeral, but no pomp and state were to be used. A coach brought up the body, which was laid the first night in the king's bed, and afterwards removed to the deanery. Four peers, who had been of his chamber, were permitted to attend as witnesses; but St. George's choir and chapel were so stript and changed, that neither peer nor Governor could find the royal vault. At last a man turned up in the town, who said he knew the stone over Henry the Eighth's grave. That vault was opened and the coffin lowered. Juxon was present, with his service-book, ready to recite his prayer, but Whichcot interfered. 'The Book of Common Prayer is put down,' he said, and not one word was suffered to be read. Some sobs were heard, some tears were shed, and the last mourners left the vault. A silver plate, bearing the legend:

KING CHARLES,

1648,

glistened on the coffin-lid. A sexton shovelled in the earth; and when the hole was filled, and the stones laid down, Whichcot turned the witnesses out, shut up the choir, and carried off the keys.

St. George's choir and chapel were deserted shrines.

But only for a time. The tide was on the turn, soon to flow back, each year with an increasing weight. Six weeks of noble patience had made amends for many faults. Calm, gracious, suffering, he had won the hearts of men and women, till they wondered how he could have lost his way. If he had fled from Bagshot Lodge, got over into France, and lived for twenty years in exile and intrigue, he might have seemed an ordinary man, no better and no worse than the princes who have lost their crowns—his house without a halo, and his family without a hope.

The martyr's march from St. James's palace to St. George's chapel, left a pathway open for his son:—to follow, when the sword had done the sword's appointed work.

CHAPTER XXVIII.

CUTTING DOWN.

1649.

ON the night of the king's execution, an alarm was raised in the Upper ward that two prisoners had escaped; one being James, called duke of Hamilton in the Scottish peerage, and the second, Henry, baron Loughborough, in the English peerage. In the darkness and confusion they had broken their parole and fled.

Whichcot was quickly on the spot; but for the night, at least, his two great captives were beyond his reach.

James, called duke of Hamilton in the Scottish peerage, and earl of Cambridge in the English peerage, had led the Scottish army into England; fallen in with Cromwell and the Ironsides at Preston Moor, been cut in pieces, straggled with a remnant of his horse to Uttoxeter, given himself up, been taken to Ashby de la Zouch, and in a little time brought up to Windsor, here to be kept, by order of the House of Commons, a ' close prisoner ' till his fine of one hundred thousand pounds had been paid.

Henry Hastings, lord Loughborough, brother of Ferdinando, earl of Huntingdon, was one of a band of royalist peers and knights who had made the very last stand that was ever to be made in arms for Charles. When Langhorne rose at Pembroke, and Hamilton crossed the border, many of the shires had risen against the Ironsides. Leicester, Kent, and Essex, were especially disturbed. Loughborough took the field in Leicester, Goring in Kent, Capel in Essex ; but the Ironside armies were too strong to be pressed back. Marching from Windsor, on what proved to be his last compaign, Fairfax struck out so heavily that none of the royalists were able to keep the field. One by one, the chiefs were driven on Colchester, pushed into the castle, and assaulted with such energy that they yielded up their swords. Lucas and Lisle had been shot in the ditch ; Loughborough, Goring, and Capel, had been brought to Windsor, as head-quarters of the military Power.

Their rooms were searched; Goring and Capel were secure; but Loughborough had disappeared.

As soldiers taken in the field and not yet tried, they had been kept in somewhat strict confinement. An exception had been made in favour of the duke. Fifteen days after his coming to Windsor, Hamilton's fine of a hundred thousand pounds, and the order for his close imprisonment, had been revoked. Placed in free custody on parole, he was allowed the freedom of his ward, and even of the park. Why he had been indulged so much, was one of the state secrets known to Cromwell and himself.

One of the richest peers in Scotland, Hamilton was a son of that marquis of Hamilton who had been created baron Ennerdale and earl of Cambridge by James the First. Charles had made him a duke, but he had done so after the war began, so that the higher title was not recognised in the English camp. At Windsor he was either known as earl of Cambridge or marquis of Hamilton; honours which he had inherited in his birth.

No person of that period gave the world more trouble to decipher; no one was able to guess his motives or explain his actions. On the surface, Hamilton appeared a mass of contradictions, not to be reconciled by the wit of man. His votes were rarely in accordance with his words; his deeds were never in accordance with his votes. At court, he had always played the courtier; while in kirk and parliament he had always been a covenanter. On the field of English politics, he had taken every side; not turn by turn, like Goring and Holland, but every side at once. With more or less reserve, he had claimed fellowship with Charles and the Cavaliers, with Essex and the Roundheads, with Cromwell and the Ironsides. He was one with church and sect, with king and parliament, with moderate and extreme. Charles had believed in him; Cromwell had made much of him. Before the sword was drawn, he had shouted for prerogative at Windsor, and voted for privilege at Westminster. From every side he had taken black mail, and always in enormous sums. One theory of his conduct was, that he cared for nothing but money; a second, that he aimed at the Scottish, if not the English crown. Though near of kin to Charles, his lips had framed the famous sentence: 'It will never be well so long as a Stuart is left alive.' The king, who had not only made him duke, but promised him a princess for a wife, was slow to see his turpitude, but at last his eyes were opened: 'He shall cousin and re-cousin me no more.' Arrested and found guilty of betraying the king, he had been sent to Exeter and Pendennis, from which he was afterwards removed to St. Michael's Mount.

There he had been found by Cromwell, and enlarged as one who had suffered in the cause. Being free to renew his plots, he had returned to court, regained his influence over Charles, and worked against him more than ever—in the dark. He, more than any other man, had ruined the king's affairs in Edinburgh. When Charles was sold, no man had taken a blacker part in the sale than he. Then the last scale had fallen from his master's eyes. Hearing in the Isle of Wight that forty thousand Scots were marching to his aid, the king inquired, 'Who leads them?' One of his majesty's attendants said: 'The duke of Hamilton.' Sighing in the bitterness of his heart, the royal captive murmured : 'Nay, if he leads them, there is no good to be done for me.'

The king was right. No good was done for him by Hamilton. The Scots were beaten and dispersed ; not without suspicion of foul play, and the payment of yet more black mail.

Windsor was all astir that winter night. Every messenger from London brought in details of the king's execution, stirring men's passions to their lowest depths. The soldiers heard of their Lord-General and his lieutenant being no longer in accord. Fairfax stood aloof, regarding the king's trial and execution as a bad business. Lady Fairfax's words, spoken in the open court, were passing from lip to lip. 'People of England!' 'Not a hundredth part of them.' Her words were felt to be the words in season; words which threw into audible shape the thought lying hidden in a multitude of minds. Everyone was excited by the day's event. If the Lord-General disapproved, who could be sure that what they had been doing was approved by Heaven?

In the confusion of that moment, Hamilton and Loughborough found a door left open, and, in spite of their plighted words, they had stolen away, unseen by Whichcot's men.

Aware that he might have to answer for the safety of his prisoners with his head, Whichcot wrote in haste to Cromwell, and at midnight his messengers were on the road. Cromwell was not only master, but appeared to have some understanding with the fugitive duke. Not many days ago, he had come to Windsor for a personal interview. The prisoner and his visitor had been closeted in secret: but the fact was known that Cromwell held out hopes of favour to the duke on certain terms, and that he left him in a friendly manner, after praying him to consider well of his reply. How the case stood between them Whichcot could only guess.

Between three and four o'clock, the messengers arrived at Cromwell's door. This was no business to be slighted, and the clerks were instantly at work. Warrants were issued for the duke's arrest; roads and ports were stopped; and a reward of five hundred pounds was offered for the fugitive. One of the messengers stopped at the post in Southwark, and spread the story of the duke's escape. Some troopers, who had overheard his story, found a man shortly afterwards knocking at an inn gate. They asked him who he was, and what he wanted in that place. He said he was a poor man, going down to Dover in the carrier's waggon, and had come to seek his carrier in that inn-yard. One of the soldiers, looking at him keenly, said: 'Methinks you are a Scot; methinks I have seen you in Hamilton's army.' This, the duke denied. Another soldier spoke out plainly. He said the man, although disguised, was no other than the duke himself. He knew his face, for he was present at the time when he was taken. That he had escaped from Windsor, they had just been told. On searching him, they found forty pounds in gold, a diamond ring worth a hundred pounds, and other articles. Here was evidence that he was not what he pretended; a poor man seeking for a passage by the Dover cart. Leading him to a boat, they carried him across the river to Whitehall.

Loughborough got away. Wiser than Hamilton, he hid himself for several weeks, and then crossed over in the Rotterdam boat and joined his master, now called Charles the Second, at the Hague.

By way of clearing ground for action, Cromwell was bent on cutting down a batch of royalist peers. Many great lords were at the Hague, and those who stayed in England, to preserve their coronets and estates, were dead against his policy. By purge and menace he had kept the Rump in order, but hereditary peers were not so easily managed as a tail of fanatics. In spite of warnings, they had scouted his proposals to judge and execute the king. He had usurped their power and closed their chamber, but his passions were not slaked and cooled. A batch of peers, condemned to die, as traitors to the commonwealth, might bring the obstinate lords to terms.

Four peers were in his hands—Hamilton, Holland, Capel, and Goring—who had been taken in the field, and might be put to death. Hamilton was at Whitehall, Holland at Warwick, Capel at Windsor with Goring as his fellow-prisoner. Cromwell had hopes that Hamilton might betray the lords who had invited him to invade the kingdom with his Scottish hosts. All day and night his officers were closeted with the duke. What was his answer to the offers made to him at Windsor?

On the following day, Capel and Goring were removed from Windsor to the Tower; from which Capel got away by dropping from the wall and wading through the moat: but, being taken by a waterman on the river, was again secured. Secret evidence satisfied the court. Pleading his Scottish birth, Hamilton claimed to be tried by a Scottish court: but he was overruled on the ground that he was an English peer and an owner of English lands. Whichcot proved that he had broken prison, after pledging his word of honour. He denied the fact, and offered to prove his truth by single combat; but the court decided that his parole had been given.　He was condemned to die. Holland, Capel, Goring, followed, and were all condemned to die; unless the Rump, in whom the gift of mercy lay, should be moved to interpose.

One of the peers was saved.　For Hamilton and Capel, not a voice was lifted up.　The duke was understood to be left in Cromwell's hands; to kill him or to spare him, as he proved his worthiness, by giving up others to the axe.　For Goring and for Holland there were equal votes; in a chamber of forty-eight members, twenty-four voting for death and life.　In each case, Lenthall had to cast the die.　At some time in their early days, Goring had done him some small kindness, and the memory of that act of kindness saved his life.　To Holland he voted 'death.'

Crowning his life with a final contradiction, Hamilton walked to the block, refused the terms of freedom, laid down his head, and died.

CHAPTER XXIX.

WINDSOR UNCROWNED.

1649–60.

An empty house, a ruined park, and a deserted shrine, Windsor was no bad picture of the state of England at the moment when the king and kingdom fell together, and a commonwealth was proclaimed at the Castle gate.

The King's house was a wreck; the fanatic, the pilferer, and the squatter, having been at work. Elizabeth's theatre was gone; the private chapel was stripped of its sacred furnishings; hall and gallery were spoiled; St. George's hall being stripped of its knightly shields, the king's gallery of its cabinets and works of art. Tudor tower and secret room were closed. Paupers had squatted in many of the towers and cabinets. Outside, the ruin was no less complete. The stand and rails were broken down. Much of the timber had been cut and sold; even the leaden pipes, which brought in water from distant springs, had been taken up. Red and fallow deer were gone. The keeper's lodge, close by Elizabeth's walk, had been destroyed.

Inside and out, Windsor was such a ruin, that the question was debated in the House of Commons whether both park and house should not be sold. One vote was carried against the sale, a second vote for the sale. Proposal followed on proposal. Some members dwelt on the shame of vending the home of Elizabeth, Harry of Agincourt, and Edward the Third; the hunting-ground of Edward the Confessor, of St. Edmund, and of other Saxon kings. These men were answered by enthusiasts, who declared that commonwealths require no royal palaces, no royal hunting-grounds. At length a compromise was made, the lots being separated into house and park. The house was kept; the park was sold :—including the Fairy dell and the Hunter's oak.

St. George's choir was closed, and Christopher Whichcot, governor of the Castle, hung the keys in his sleeping-room. Dean, canons, choristers, knew their places on the hill no more. The altars were defaced, the hatchments overturned, the communion-table carted off. Hugh Peters, regimental gospeller of Windsor, cared no more for 'oyster-benches' than Hugh Weston, catholic dean of Windsor, had cared for them in Queen Mary's time. Not only was the shrine dismantled, but the saint himself was stricken from the calendar. No other saints were tolerated save the saints of God. Except his cross, nothing of the saint was spared; the barred white flag of Sluys and Agincourt; which floated from the keep—less as an emblem of the cross than of the sword.

A commonwealth was proclaimed.

At once the strife broke out. Waller, with Major-general Browne, Sir John Clotworthy, and many more, declared against the change of government. Next to Manchester, Waller was the most eminent captain of the earlier period of the war now left alive. A man of family and fortune, and a member of the House of Commons, his voice was loud and his opinion strong. He had opposed the king's trial and execution; he now opposed the fall of monarchy. In other days he had outrun Essex, now he saw himself outrun by Cromwell and his peers. With him, as with so many more, the sword had broken in his hand. Waller, Browne, Clotworthy, were arrested, brought to head-quarters, and secured at Windsor under Harrison's charge. Waller reviewed the past, and sought the prisoner's solace in his pen. 'I look on the present alteration of government as a treasonable act. . . . If I be continued in prison it shall not trouble me. I have lived in prison ever since I was born: my body is no other to me than a prison, and a worse prison than that wherein I lie. I am both a prison and a prisoner to myself. I may be shut up, but God cannot be shut out.'

His strength was put to the severest tests. More than once he was removed from Windsor to other castles, and brought back again. In the same lofty strain he wrote: 'I thank God I can despise the worst. I have weighed poverty and banishment, imprisonment and death, and I have found them light in the balance. I know how to want, and how to abound. I can be at home, abroad, and a free man, in a prison. I can find life in death.'

A man like Waller could be locked up, but he could never be subdued; and those who shared his opinions held to them all the stronger for his sake.

The Windsor army found itself more and more

alone ; grim, solid, irresistible, yet more and more alone.

A commonwealth was proclaimed. What commonwealth ?—whose commonwealth? Was this new government a government of the English people, by the English people? No, replied the victors, who had certainly not shed their blood to retire, and let affairs go on by Yea and Nay. A vast majority of the people wanted peace and liberty, but peace and liberty as they existed in the times of Queen Elizabeth. That was no theory favoured by the Saints, who meant to have a commonwealth of the godly—of the chosen—men who were worthy of the Cause, and who had been faithful to the end.

The generals at head-quarters were divided; Fairfax thinking they had gone too far, Cromwell protesting they had not gone far enough. The moderate officers were with Fairfax, the immoderate were with Cromwell. In the rank and file, no less than in the officers' quarters, feuds sprang up. If free-born Englishmen required no kings, why should they have lord-generals and lieutenant-generals? If the question rose, 'Cæsar or nothing ?' they were ready to reply, ' Republic or nothing.' Here the Levellers took up their ground and raised their cry: 'No parks, no chases, no enclosures; no kings, no magistrates, no general officers.' These seekers after truth stuck ribands in their hats. They had to be revised with sword and shot.

Ireland began to stir, and troops were needed from head-quarters to repress an insurrection in that country. Cromwell came to Windsor to consult the General, who was well content to let him take that charge. The House appointed Cromwell general for Ireland, leaving Fairfax generalissimo for the commonwealth. Starting from Windsor, Cromwell marched towards Milford Haven, taking Hugh Peters for his prophet, and eighty captains and colonels for a body-guard; and having crossed the sea, swept through the Irish counties as he had formerly swept through the English counties. For the first time in their history, the kernes were thoroughly cut down.

As Irish chief and kerne fell back, the Scottish chiefs and clans sprang forward; Charles the Second being invited over, sworn to the covenant, and proclaimed their king. Fairfax declined to march against them. He had lost his confidence in the sword as an interpreter of the divine will. His heart was not with the new government, and he had no desire to take the field against a second king. Rather than fight again, he resigned his post. Windsor saw the Lord-General's face no more. Henceforward, Cromwell held the sword.

Cromwell felt no doubts. For him, success was right, and victory 'the providence of God.'

Dunbar followed; after Dunbar, Worcester. Then the sword was sheathed; nothing more being left for it to do. England lay still; awed into silence and submission by an overmastering military power. Hugh Peters whispered to himself: 'This man will yet be king.'

One duke, seven earls, with many lords and gentlemen of station, fell into Cromwell's hands at Worcester. Three of the Scottish earls, Kelly, Lauderdale, and Rothes, were brought to Windsor, where they shared the prison lodgings of Waller and the English generals. In driving through Cornhill, Lauderdale's coach was stopped, when a carter, peeping in at the window, snarled: 'Oh, my lord! You are welcome to London, I protest! Off goes your head, round as a hoop!' The prisoner laughed, and jogged along. He and his fellows pined in their imprisonment for the next nine years. When Charles came back, he was released; living to become an English earl and a Scottish duke, and to play his part in the second and final act of the Divine Catastrophe.

The commonwealth was abolished; a Protectorate declared.

Under the new system, Windsor was made 'a garrison.' The town was disfranchised. Headquarters were removed to Westminster. St. George's keep became a military jail.

'January 30 : Mr. Feak and Mr. Simpson sent prisoners to Windsor Castle : ' so, in Whitelock, under date. Feak was a Saint, eager to do away with lord-generals, lord-lieutenants, and all other mundane lordships, and to inaugurate the Reign of Christ. His conventicle, which he called Christ Church, stood in Blackfriars, and was the rallying-ground for Sunday sermon and Monday lecture of the more exalted sectaries. Harrison, and other officers of the army, were amongst his hearers. Feak had borne the commonwealth impatiently, as a postponement of the Reign of Christ ; and when the commonwealth gave place to the protectorate, he broke all bounds. Cromwell, he announced from the pulpit, was the 'man of sin,' the 'old dragon.' Cromwell was angry, but the man could not be silenced legally. The church was open, and the preacher licensed, under an act of parliament which Cromwell's council had no power to set aside. Nothing but force would serve; and some of Cromwell's council were not sure that even force would serve. At Temple Bar, Cheapside, and the Exchange, the proclamation was received with ridicule. Except the soldiers, no one raised a shout for Oliver. Men listened to the heralds, and walked away in scorn. At Temple Bar, one citizen asked: 'What is the matter?' One of the troopers answered, 'They are proclaiming the Lord Protector.' 'Protector?' sneered the citizen, 'he protects none but such rogues as thou art!' The soldier struck him. Rushing at the mounted man, the citizen pulled him from his horse, fought with him, drubbed him soundly, and marched away unhurt. A great crowd stood around, who laughed, and cheered the citizen. Yet some of the council sat on their horses, and observed that scene.

Cromwell sent for Feak, and told him that his attacks on the government gave confidence to the enemy abroad and at home, and brought parliament into contempt. Feak answered: 'Let your words and mine be recorded in heaven.' Feak declared that not his words, but Cromwell's assumption of exorbitant power, had caused the disorder. 'When I heard you begin with a record in heaven,' said the Lord Protector, 'I did not expect you would tell such a lie on earth.' He assured the preacher that if he should be harder pressed by the enemy than he had been, he might have to begin with him. On leaving the Protector, Feak inquired of Harrison whether *he* accepted the Protectorate? Harrison replied with an emphatic 'No;' he recognised no king save Christ. Speaking in his pulpit, Feak declared the Lord Protector the most dissembling and most perjured villain in the world. Looking at his audience, he continued: 'If he have any friends here, I desire that they will go and tell him what I have said.' Glancing at the last Lord Protector, the Anabaptist said: 'His reign shall be but short; he shall be served worse than that great tyrant; he being as bad, if not worse, than Somerset.'

Harrison and Feak were called into Cromwell's presence. They maintained their opposition to the new Protectorate. Harrison was dismissed the service; Feak was committed to Windsor Castle; each appealing to the law against the sword.

CHAPTER XXX.

A 'MERRY' CÆSAR.

1660-70.

NOT till the brain that fashioned, and the hand that guided, the victorious army were at rest, was England herself again ; free to go back on her old lines, and to adopt the order of her choice. But on the death of Oliver everything was changed. The sword dropped down—four feet of tempered steel ; helmet and breast-plate sank into articles of a soldier's dress ; the soul that quickened them into a living force was gone.

No nation loves heroic rule, except in times of peril ; and, the danger being past, no nation feels much patience with heroic guides. Cromwell was never loved. The people bore his rule, because they found in him a statesman worthy of a land which had produced Elizabeth and Edward the Third. Under his government, their greatness was revived ; once more they were objects of attention to surrounding courts ; their sea-generals flaunting the red cross in seas from which they had been excluded since the Tudor times. Yet Oliver's government was endured, and nothing more. In spite of genius, valour, and prosperity, the Ironside captain failed to reach the national heart.

At Windsor, as in other parts, his presence was a working power. As Lord Protector, he re-bought the Little park ; he planted and improved the forest ; he opened St. George's chapel for public worship ; he kept an eye on the college lands ; he partially restored the royal house. Yet no one cared for him :—he was too great, too lofty, too austere. Windsor, in truth, was sick of his heroic work. The strain had been too hard, and had endured too long. Men wanted cakes and ale. Heroic? Yea ; but Windsor wanted to be free. Waller had said in his Windsor cell, that under Charles, men talked of being slaves when they were free ; while under Oliver, they talked of being free while they were slaves. What Waller said, the burgesses had begun to feel. For fifteen years, the Ironsides had eaten into their souls. No English town had seen so much of them as Windsor, and no English town gave warmer welcome to their enemy, the returning prince.

Droll were the forms in which their loyalty came out.

When writs were issued for a 'free parliament,' Windsor elected Roger Palmer, barrister-at-law, to give her voice for calling in King Charles. Palmer was the husband of a fair woman, soon to be known, at Windsor and elsewhere, as Lady Castlemaine. A frantic royalist, Palmer had seen the king, had lent him money, and had introduced his wife. Taking the money and the lady, Cæsar had sent the gentleman back to Windsor, where he had some secret friends, to manage his affairs. Galland, a tavern keeper, happened to be mayor; lawyer and host soon came to terms; and though some burgesses opposed them, Palmer was returned. Riding up to Westminster, this husband of a fair wife voted, in the name of Windsor, for his majesty's recall.

A troop of county horse rode into the town, on which Galland, in his robe of office, walked to the market cross, a trumpeter in front of him, and there proclaimed King Charles. Attended by his county horse, he marched to the bridge, where he again proclaimed King Charles. Creeping to the

Castle gates, he looked in ; when the captain bade them enter, and the zealous Galland read his pro-clamation under St. George's keep. Sixty-six shillings were drunk in sack and ale at Mr. Galland's board.

Later on, the mayor and aldermen held a feast in honour of the great event : — but at the public cost. Their loyalty rose so high, that they resolved to hold that festival once a-year ; and always at the public cost. ' Twenty pounds a-year for feast-ing—to continue seven years,' was voted by the court.

When the king returned, Windsor was herself again. The royal house was occupied. St. George's choir was opened and restored. The old flag floated from the Norman keep. Mordaunt was appointed Constable, but was afterwards replaced by Rupert. Deans, canons, choristers, appeared in their robes and surplices, and Knights of the Garter sat once more in their ancient stalls.

Men were so weary of experiments in 'freedom,' that if Charles had been either pure of life or sound of faith, he might easily have rooted his dynasty in the soil. England was not his enemy, nor the enemy of his race. To her, indeed, he was the issue of her ancient kings ; the minister and mainstay of her ancient laws. None but the sectaries were his foes, and these men had already done their best and worst. They were disarmed, dispersed, and broken up. The county bands were once more the militia of the kingdom, and the principal material power. Nothing seemed easier than to rally a majority of the people to his side. An offer like his father's, to go back, in church and state, on the condition of affairs in Queen Elizabeth's time, was all he needed to propose. But he was neither pure in life nor sound in faith. He had no thought of going back to Queen Elizabeth's time. He was a Cæsar, and he meant to rule by a supreme and sacred right, older than either English usage or English law. The only lesson he had learnt in exile was, the wisdom of enjoying the passing hour. 'Eat and drink, for to-morrow ye die.' Where he left his family legend, was in his resolve to be a merry despot, not a grave one, like his father, a morose one, like his grandfather. He had studied in a wanton school, and he arrived at Windsor with the notion that a sovereign, to be great and popular like Louis the Fourteenth, must, like Louis the Fourteenth, live the life of a Roman emperor.

Early association drew him to Windsor; but in

making the King's house his summer palace, he was thinking rather of Louis and his projects at Versailles, than of an English country house, as Windsor had been in his father's time. Except his leaning towards his mother's church, little of his majesty's youth remained. Before he came to Windsor, and revisited his mother's cabinet and chapel, he had passed that stage of personal depravity in which a man likes to recall his mother's image. He was steeped, neck-deep, in shame.

Barbara Palmer was but one of his many favourites; but his appearance in the Windsor galleries with that shameless creature, was denounced by men who smiled at ordinary breaches of the moral law. The queen was present; most of the peeresses were present; for the festival of St. George was graced by the installation of two singular knights : one being no less a person than the Danish king, the other no greater than Crofts, the king's illegimate son. Catharine was in the first year of her marriage; yet the king, her husband forced on her the evidence of his former frailties. Crofts was pretty, and she liked him as a page, but Charles had married him to Lady Ann, heiress of Buccleugh, created him baron Scott, earl of Doncaster, and duke of Monmouth, and talked of creating him prince of Wales. He seemed to pass between her offspring and the crown. Yet she received him kindly, and after dinner led him out to dance. The king came in. Monmouth held his cap in hand. Charles kissed him, and bade him don his cap; an act of rudeness, both in manner and suggestion, that caused her heart to sink. A prince of Wales should not have gone so far. Yet Catharine suffered in the woman more than in the boy. Palmer was now an Irish earl, and his abandoned partner, Lady Castlemaine. Charles had forced her company on his queen; an insult which had thrown her into fits. A pious lady, bred in a convent, she declared with sobs : 'I cannot in my conscience consent to what may give an opportunity for sin.' Cold and cynical, Charles insisted on arranging his seraglio as he pleased; and Lady Castlemaine not only came with him to Windsor, but as first lady of the queen's bed-chamber, had apartments given to her in the royal house. 'The queen is much grieved of late at the king's neglect,' notes Pepys ; 'he not having supped with her this quarter of a year, but almost every night with my Lady Castlemaine, who has been with him,' at Windsor, 'this St. George's feast, and came home with him last night.'

Some changes were required at Windsor to convert the study of Elizabeth, and the gallery of Charles the First, into the image of a French seraglio. May was employed to build, and Verrio to paint. A 'star' chamber was erected on the northern side ; a flat and hideous length of front, without one compensating line or curve. Vanity described the work as 'stately.' Stateliness was the fashion. Louis the Fourteenth's new palace at Versailles was stately ; bigness and tameness being supposed to cover up every fault. Some Gothic building of a noble period was disturbed and partially destroyed. The Norman keep was faced with brick !

Inside, the rooms and ceilings were smeared with Verrio's pinks and blues ; with gods and goddesses floating in the air ; in the king's bed-room, an allegory ; in the queen's room, an assembly of the cardinal virtues ; in the dining-hall, a banquet of the gods. Thanks to Evelyn, one true artist was employed ; and Gibbons' carvings made amends for much that was paltry and pretentious in the other work.

St. George's hall was turned into a French theatre ; tricked and altered on the caprice of French comedians ; and here the king and his concubines listened to dialogues in French, too free for audiences which heard without disgust such plays as Love in a Wood and the Country Wife.

A great seraglio, like Versailles, with kiosques and gardens round about, was Charles's idea of a summer palace; and so far as Windsor and the forest could be turned into such a residence, they were turned by his command. Lady Castlemaine and the French courtesan, given to him by Louis, had apartments in the Castle, Nell Gwyn in Burford house; while Moll Davies, and other 'beauties,' were occasionally entertained at Bagshot lodge and Cranbourne lodge. Cæsar occupied the Tudor tower. Will Chiffinch, his trusty usher, lived on the lower tier; and Madame Nun, that usher's sister, a personage of dubious calling, had apartments near the Private stair. Will's room, a handsome and 'effeminate' lounge, became one of Cæsar's hunting-grounds.

Cæsars were always penniless. Charles never had money enough, and 'want' was his excuse for doing a thousand dirty things: robbing the dock-yards; intercepting the sailors' pay; selling Dunkerque; accepting a pension from the king of France.

A Dutch fleet pushed into the Thames. England, so great under Elizabeth and under Oliver, fell into the rank of a third-rate power. Yet, wearied by heroic effort, she might have borne with her restored princes, had they but shown themselves sound in faith. Englishmen disliked subservience to the court of France ; no power on earth could reconcile them to the court of Rome.

CHAPTER XXXI.

WINDSOR CATHOLIC.

1670–87.

NEITHER Charles nor James had ever, in his heart, been sound of faith.

In his earlier days, Charles had taken the Covenant; in his later days he had sworn to observe the English Articles. Yet, at the age of thirty, he had returned to Windsor as good a Catholic as he had left it, with his mother, at the age of twelve. In public, he consented to receive the sacrament in the English form; but only after finding that his friends might otherwise be confined to those Catholic houses which had been already beaten in his cause. Those houses could do nothing more for him. The nation, and the nation only, could repress the sectaries; and he was shown, by all his reasonable councillors, that if he wanted popular support, he must rally the English people round the English church. Thus, in the fashion of his grandsire, Henri of Navarre, he made a sacrifice of his faith in order to enjoy his pleasure and preserve his crown.

Yet his arrival at Windsor was the signal for a movement in the town, which wrote its history in small things as in great. Those who welcomed a restoration of the crown, felt bound in conscience to restore the cross. In the town-books we read:

> ' Paid for setting up the king's arms, 2s. 6d.
> ' Paid towards the cross setting up, 2l. 15s.'

No bishop, no king—no cross, no crown; the two things seemed to hang by a common bar.

Allowed under their father's marriage treaty, to be reared in the faith of Rome until they were old enough to choose a creed, the two princes had been grounded by their mother's monks and women so completely, that in after years they had always kept their first impressions of religious truth : Charles, as a secret hidden from his people, though intrusted to his male and female favourites ; James, as a gift and blessing, not only privately enjoyed, but publicly proclaimed. To Charles, indeed, religion was a mask, if not a jest. He had no zeal. The catholic creed, he said, was the only creed for a gentleman ;

but in his opinion, as in that of his grandsire, no religion was worth a crown.

First and last, he was a traitor to the English church. He took a catholic wife, and, while professing to espouse her by an English rite, he secretly espoused her by a papal rite. Catharine of Braganza had come to Windsor much as Henrietta of France had come to Windsor—an emissary from the court of Rome, charged with the task of once more bending the English people under the papal yoke. 'I take God to witness,' she reported to his holiness, 'that no desire of crown or sceptre led me to become queen of England : I had no other thought than the desire of being useful to the catholic church.' Like the queen-mother, she had her chapel fitted up at Windsor; and she turned her court, so far as she had power, into a catholic court.

As with his consort, so with his concubine. Lady Castlemaine was born a Calvinist; she became a convert to the king's religion : not by any change of thought or feeling, but entirely, as she boasted, on the ground of policy. 'I have not embraced the catholic religion out of any esteem that I have for it ; but because I could not otherwise continue to be the king's mistress, and to be

the miss of State.' Her husband had already joined
the party which he took to be that of the coming
church. Some members of her family, who had
less objection to own a courtesan than an apostate,
waited on his majesty, and begged him to prevent
her yielding to her priests. Charles only laughed :
' Excuse me, I have nothing to do with women's
souls.' The queen, aware of Lady Castlemaine's
motives, was annoyed at this conversion. 'It is
not done,' she sighed, 'for conscience sake.' On
hearing of the fact, Stillingfleet observed : ' If
the church of Rome has got no more than the
church of England has lost, the matter will not be
much:'—words which were afterwards applied to
Charles himself.

A secret treaty (Dover, May, 1670), signed
between the lord of Versailles and the lord of
Windsor, bound his majesty to throw aside his
mask, and show his face to all the world as he
had shown it to Lady Castlemaine. For money
down, and the promise of a pension, Charles agreed
to make a public profession of catholicism, and to
assist his French neighbour in putting down the
Protestant Netherlands. In case of risings in the
country, caused by this apostasy, French armies
were to land in England, occupy London and

Windsor, and prevent new Ironside regiments being raised and drilled.

Charles took the money, but postponed the public declaration of his apostasy. That declaration, he had sense enough to see, would be his ruin. He never lacked an excuse for keeping any money that might reach his hand.

Once, in a penitent fit, the House of Commons voted him a sum of seventy thousand pounds to build a monument to the king, his father. Not one shilling of that vote was spent in St. George's choir. Designs were sketched, and epitaphs composed. Lindsay and Southampton were required to indicate the exact position of the royal grave; they came to Windsor and affected to search the choir. Their presence was a farce. The grave was known, and since the Restoration had been a common show. Evelyn had seen it; Pepys had seen it; every visitor in the choir had seen it. Lindsay and Southampton knew it well, for they were present when the coffin had been lowered into the vault. Yet they were said to have reported that the martyr's grave could not be found. Designs and epitaphs were laid aside, and penniless Cæsar scattered that pious fund among his Castlemaines and Gwyns.

Not till he was on his death-bed, was his majesty brave enough to announce his creed, and only then, to the innermost circle of his court.

During his reign, a statue was erected to him in the upper ward ; a mounted Cæsar, cast in metal, with his name conspicuous on a shield :

CAROLO SECUNDO,

REGUM OPTIMO

DOMINO SUO CLEMENTISSIMO

TOBIAS RUSTAT

HANC EFFIGIEM HUMILIME

DEDIT ET DEDICAVIT

ANNO DOMINI MDCLXXX.

This statue was erected and dedicated by a page of the back-stairs : the most lucrative office in Cæsar's gift.

Bolder than his brother, James the Second avowed his creed. The member of his family whom the last of the royal Stuarts most admired, was his ancestress, Mary, queen of Scots. She never bent, he said ; and he, her offspring, would never bend. 'My father yielded, and he lost his life.' James seemed to have forgotten, that though

Mary had not bent, she had been driven from her country by her outraged people, and had ultimately lost her head. His reverence for that woman was so great, that when his children died in infancy, he opened her grave, and laid them by her side. For him she was a saint, whose ashes purified the ground. Like her, he staked his crown and dynasty on the issue of a fight between a liberal people and a fanatical prince.

Standing in the country, and enclosed by walls and gates, Windsor appeared to him a safer theatre for his experiment than a palace like Whitehall, surrounded by the population of two cities, and exposed to an attack by river, street, and park. Windsor was therefore taken as his place of arms; and during his three years' reign, the King's house and St. George's choir became head-quarters of the catholic church.

James had never ceased to be a catholic; but before the Restoration, and for some time after that event, his faith had been concealed. His first wife, Lady Anne, had been a convert to his church; but her conversion had been kept a secret, in the interest of her daughters, the Princess Mary and the Princess Anne. The young princesses, he supposed, were catholics; but he had suffered them to take the English sacraments in deference to their prospects in the world ; Mary being married to William of Orange, and Anne to George of Denmark. Like the king, his brother, James had taken for a second wife a catholic ; eager to restore the unity of Rome at the expense of English liberty and law. While she was simply duchess of York, Mary of Modena had played the lamb. No voice was meeker than her own ; few minds more tolerant than her own. She was supposed to exercise a softening influence over the fanatical duke. But they were hardly on the throne, before both duke and duchess threw away their masks. Lord Castlemaine was sent to Rome ; Cardinal D'Adda was received as nuncio. Father Petre, the famous Jesuit, and Father Ellis, the no less famous Benedictine, were installed at the King's house as chaplains and advisers. Petre was of catholic blood, Ellis of evangelical blood; both had been educated in the Jesuit schools. Ellis was a stolen child ; having been kidnapped from Westminster school, conveyed, without the knowledge of his family, to St. Omers, and brought up as a catholic priest. He was a pleasant, humorous man, of greater talent, but of far less zeal, than Petre. While at St. Omers, he had been known as 'jolly Phil ;'

but he had chosen to become a Benedictine rather than a Jesuit. James, who saw in him the convert and man of talent, chose him as leader of his crusade. Windsor was appointed for the scene; king, queen, and court were present, and the Benedictine preached a sermon in St. George's chapel:—the first distinctly catholic sermon since Spalatro's time. An eas-going fellow, Ellis was rather moderate in his views; but on this occasion he was bound to satisfy the king and queen. Taking for his text these words: 'Thou shalt love the Lord thy God with all thy heart, and with all thy soul, and with all thy mind,' he proved, to the king's satisfaction—first, that the church of England was not a church; second, that no man could be saved except within the fold of Rome. Spalatro had never gone so far as Father Ellis : but Windsor under James the Second was not so timid in her papistry, as Windsor in the time of James the First.

Armed with the authority of his Benedictine monk, James undertook, by fraud and violence, to overturn the fabric of what he heard was not a church, and had no power to save men's souls. He dissolved parliaments, suspended the penal laws, imprisoned bishops, seized the revenues of colleges, and raised an army under the command of Louis de Duras, a French adventurer, now earl of Feversham and chamberlain to the queen. Windsor was the head-quarters of these iniquities. The king began to touch for scrofula; he discharged the dean from his attendance; he filled his house with monks and priests, and introduced once more the Latin language and the Roman rite. A state reception was arranged for D'Adda, and though many Englishmen objected to the act, the king bore down their opposition with a heavy hand. Charles, duke of Somerset, lord of the bed-chamber, was at Windsor with the king. James wished him to attend the nuncio; Somerset begged to be excused. James insisted on knowing why, saying: 'I thought, my lord, that I was doing you a great honour, in appointing you to escort the minister of the first of crowned heads.'

Somerset answered: 'Sir, I am advised not to do it, for the act is treason.'

'Who gave you that advice?' inquired the king.

Somerset declined to name his friend.

'It is some Whig councillor,' retorted James.

Somerset would say no more.

'I will make you fear me,' the king went

on: ' do you not know that I am above the law?'

Somerset bowed. 'Your majesty may be above the law, but I am not.' ·

Dunbarton, a catholic, was appointed to succeed the duke. One of the bystanders snarled, ' A duke of Somerset once put out the Pope, and now the Pope has put out the duke of Somerset.'

Two chairs of state were placed in St. George's Hall. Grafton, the second son of Lady Castlemaine, brought up the procession. D'Adda, seated with Grafton and a master of the ceremonies, came first in a royal coach. Two coaches followed, filled with priests ; thirty-four coaches followed, with the principal ministers of state and officers of the royal household. Two bishops figured on the scene. They entered by the great gate, crossed the guard-room, and entered St. George's Hall. The king and queen received the nuncio standing, as the representative of the highest power on earth.

All England stood aghast.

CHAPTER XXXII.

THE CATASTROPHE.

1688–9.

SUCH doings brought on the Catastrophe.

A dozen plots were formed. Argyll invaded Scotland ; Monmouth invaded England. These attempts to raise an insurrection failed; because, in spite of deep repugnance to such scenes as those at Windsor, people still shrank from an appeal to arms. That method had been tried; few thought that public grievances could be remedied by force. To drive out James in order to bring in new Cromwells, seemed a doubtful gain ; assuredly not worth the havoc of a second civil war. They chose to wait. James had no son; the catholic line would end with him. Mary, his daughter, was a protestant, united to a protestant prince. In her, the popular fancy saw the promise of a new Elizabeth ; in her, and in her husband, they had reason to expect a remedy in right and law.

One day, a son was born, or was reported to be born. The child was brought to Windsor, and established in the house of Nell Gwyn. D'Adda, the papal nuncio, and Catharine of Braganza, were his sponsors, and the ceremony was conducted with the utmost splendour of the catholic rite.

By this event, everything was changed. England had now the prospect of a papist line of kings, and a perpetual strife between the country and the crown.

Was no deliverer yet in sight?

Yes ; the man of destiny, who was to end this drama and complete the Divine Catastrophe, lay nigh at hand.

That little girl, who had said at Windsor, ' Take me to mass, I shall be glad to go,' and who had knelt throughout the service in her mother's chapel, had been rescued by her marriage from all chance of falling into Romish ways. Her only offspring was a son, born after her husband's death. This son—William of Orange—stood, next after James's children, in direct succession to the English throne. By birth a Calvinist, he sympathised with those who regarded the church of England as an excellent pattern of a national church. He differed from them in his carelessness about episcopal orders; but with moderate puritans, like Essex and Manchester, he had almost everything in common. Thus, he stood nearer to the heart of England than any other prince who boasted of pretensions to the crown. If he had been ten years older, and if Charles, while yet in exile, had shown himself an obstinate catholic, he might have been restored instead of Charles and James. Since then, his claims had been strengthened by his marriage to his cousin, Princess Mary.

When a son was born, the catholic court at Windsor watched this man's proceedings with alarm. James disliked him, both on personal and on public grounds. A cold and silent man, even for a Hollander, William was reported to neglect his English bride. The story was not true. In feeble health, he was disposed to brood and mope; and his brick barrack at the Hague, bordered by sombre trees and stagnant pools, had none of the festive airs of Windsor and Whitehall. Yet Mary loved him in the face of his defects. She saw, as other people saw, the heroic side of his great character. As captain and as councillor, William had few equals. An ambition, knowing no limits, fed itself on a perfect consciousness of his birthright in the English crown. James disliked him for his religion, and for the popularity which his religion brought him ; seeing with a jaundiced eye that he was popular in England mainly on the ground of being the most formidable enemy of the Roman church.

This hatred of his nephew was intensified in James's heart by the birth of his son and heir. Hardly one Englishman in ten acknowledged the brat in Nell Gwyn's house to be his son. Men whispered that he was a spurious child, brought in by Jesuits and Italian nurses, to deprive the king's daughters of their rights. Anne professed to have the fullest evidence of the fraud. She was mistaken in her proofs, but her mistake was shared not only by the multitude, but by many of those who stood in near relations to the court. Not so the couple at the Hague. William had so little thought of fraud, that he sent his agent, Zulestein, to congratulate his uncle on the advent of a prince. Not until Zulestein's arrival in England, was he made aware that everyone was crying out ' foul play,' and calling on him to cross the sea, and do what might be done to save the liberties and religion of the land in which he had such imminent claims.

William prepared to sail. It was a painful task to move against his father-in-law; but if England were to be preserved from civil war, some protestant and popular prince must lend his hand. Two other princes had some show of right in law; George of Denmark and George of Hanover; and if he dropt his claim, they might have found the kingdom at his back.

James drove in to Windsor with the queen and prince, and here he meant to make his stand. Was he to call a parliament or not? He hated parliaments, and his sycophants knew the bitterness of that hate. Jeffreys, his chancellor, dissuaded him; Petre, his privy councillor, dissuaded him. These members of his council shared the innermost secrets of his heart. They also knew that no device, no bribery, no intimidation, could collect a parliament in Westminster that would not drive his popish ministers from the royal house. Therefore, they bade him trust in Feversham's sword. James murmured that he saw no help. London was up behind him, with the citizens out, and everything at stake. William proposed a parliament: everybody yelled 'A parliament—a free parliament!' At Windsor, the state of things reminded men of Digby's time; except that in Digby's time, the crown was not committed openly to the church of Rome. 'I will have a parliament,' sighed the king in his despair, and Jeffreys received his orders to prepare the writs. Petre, at the same time, was warned to be in readiness for flight—he and the baby-prince.

William landed at Torbay, and set his march towards Windsor, as the king's head-quarters. James threw out his troops towards Salisbury, under Feversham, hoping to cut him off. Leaving the queen and prince at Windsor, but taking George of Denmark with him, James set out for Salisbury, attended by a brilliant staff. Some days were wasted in parade. Feversham had no ability for his work ; and men like Churchill, who had ability for the work, were waiting for an opportunity to desert. Day after day, night after night, the king was told of officers and peers going over to his enemy. Three regiments went over at a stroke. Manchester joined the prince. Even George of Denmark stole away. He learned that his base-nephew Grafton, and his creature Churchhill, had formed a plot to carry him off and surrender him to the prince of Orange.

Petre, who was at Windsor with the baby-prince, received an order to remove him secretly, taking with him only his governess and his foreign nurse. Snatched up by the Jesuit and his nurse, the child was borne away, to start that wandering life, which, ebbing and flowing for nearly eighty years, was at last to close in the great city for which he sacrificed his crown.

Hardly any blood was drawn. There was, in truth, no need to draw the sword; the country was of one opinion; all except a knot of catholics here and there—men who could do nothing of themselves. The policy of William was a 'bloodless change;' the plan, to turn and push the king backward, till he found his personal safety in a boat. Close in James's rear, as he retired from Salisbury, William entered. Here he was joined by Clarendon, Oxford, and many other peers, and setting forth again, moved, amidst ever-increasing acclamations, to Oxford, Wallingford, and Windsor; —once again head-quarters of the Good Old Cause.

Unable to regain Windsor, James fell back on London. Here his consort quitted him, much as the queen, his mother, had quitted her consort, Charles the First, at Hampton Court.

Next day, the king fled also; after throwing the Great Seal into the Thames, burning the writs for a new parliament, and ordering Feversham to disband the guard. Met by foul weather, he was thrown on shore, buffeted and robbed, and forced to retrace his steps.

What next? William had no desire to drive him hard ; he only wished to squeeze him out, and end his reign without loss of life. James sent Feversham to Windsor with a note, inviting William to a conference, and offering him St. James's palace for a lodging. William regarded Feversham with distrust, partly for his French extraction, partly for his many base compliances with the king. William refused to see him. What was he about ? He had brought a letter from the king, which would require an answer. William was thinking of his infamy in disbanding the guard, and turning them adrift in the darkness of a winter night, to the great peril of the king's capital. 'That is high treason,' said the prince, and ordered Feversham into arrest. This blow was widely felt. James was not yet deposed, and Feversham was his general. To disband the guard, however infamous an act, was certainly within his power. Yet William lodged him in a chamber of St. George's keep, declaring that he held him prisoner of the state, till he produced the actual order of the king.

Zulestein rode from Windsor with his answer

to the king. James must retire ; William would not enter London till the king had left. Next day, Clarendon, Rochester, and other lords arrived at Windsor. William was at church. Clarendon went into his bed-chamber, where he found Bentinck, the prince's most confidential man. William occupied Will Chiffinch's rooms, on the lower tier of the Tudor tower ; Bentinck had the duchess of Portsmouth's rooms. They talked of Feversham. Clarendon asked him the meaning of that arrest ; Bentinck was silent. When Clarendon pressed, he answered with a shrug : ' Alas ! my lord.' Clarendon confessed that he was strangely startled, but the silent Dutchman said no more. When the prince came in from church, he spoke to Clarendon kindly, but was cold and rude to his brother Rochester. These trimmers hardly understood the prince. At dinner in the deanery, Clarendon expressed his wonder why a messenger from the king, who brought a civil message from his majesty, inviting the prince to town, should be imprisoned in St. George's keep. Burnet, who was present, laughed. The talk grew perilous. The bishop of St. Asaph argued, that, by leaving London, James had ceded his crown. ' What do you mean ?' demanded Clarendon. ' It can be nothing but a cession of the crown,' replied the bishop, unabashed. The peer was still more shocked. James was his brother-in-law, and much of the prosperity of his family seemed to be bound up with James. These interests blinded him to the position of events. The truth was, William's arrest of Feversham was an act of state : useful, as a by-blow, to alarm the king. Feversham struck down, no other captain would be likely to take his place.

A council was convened at Windsor. Most of the great peers were present. The question to be debated was : what shall be done with James? William retired to his apartments, and Halifax assumed the chair. The peers agreed that James must quit Whitehall ; they thought of Ham, and other manors on the Thames. Halifax repaired to the prince, and told him what they had agreed. The message was drawn up. ' Whom shall we send with it?' asked the prince. 'Ought it not,' inquired Halifax, 'to be conveyed by one of your highness's officers?' 'Nay, my lord, by your favour,' answered William ; 'it is sent by the advice of your lordships, and some of you ought to carry it.' Halifax and two other lords got into their coaches, and drove to London. Middleton, the king's chamberlain, received them in the ante-room. The king had gone to bed, and might not be disturbed ; they told him they must see the king at once. Middleton slipped into the closet, and presently returned to say the king would see them. On entering, they found his majesty in bed, ill, and in the lowest spirits. On saying that the prince was coming, they asked him, for his personal safety, to retire, and offered him Lauderdale's house at Ham. 'Must this be done at once?' the king inquired. They answered, he might take his sleep out, and on saying so, they withdrew. Middleton followed them to the ante-room, to ask him if he might go to Rochester instead of Ham. Ham was a cold, damp place. William, who only wished him to be gone—committing what was legally 'an act of desertion'—put no obstacle in his way. Next morning he retired, and Windsor saw his face no more ; the Divine Catastrophe was complete.

On New Year's eve, William paid a public visit to the queen-dowager, Catharine of Braganza ; and, among other chit-chat, asked her how she passed her time, and whether she still enjoyed her game of basset? She had not played a game, she said, since the loss of her chamberlain. William took her hint. 'If that be so, I will not interrupt your majesty's diversions.' On the following day, Feversham was released ;—the last State prisoner of St. George's keep.

CHAPTER XXXIII.

DOMESTIC LIFE.

1696–1796.

From the moment of Feversham's liberation from St. George's keep, Windsor ceases to be heroic, and becomes domestic.

Henceforth, the history is that of a country-house; a country-house beyond example stately and picturesque, as royal residence should be; but still, the homestead of a family, more or less united in all its parts; not a fortress, armed against this or that party in the kingdom; not the head-quarters of either a mutiny against the law, or of an insurrection against the crown. It is a house in which artists painted, musicians played, and architects wrought; in which ladies lived, children prattled, and old men dozed; in which knights were made, ambassadors heard, and royal visitors received. The charm of Windsor is that of family life.

Two of these scenes have made themselves abiding-places in the memory of men.

In the first scene, the principal figure is a little child ; in the second scene, that of an old man.

The child is Willie, duke of Gloucester, infant son of queen Anne ; a bright and pretty boy, with Danish blood in his young veins, like that of the unforgotten Henry, prince of Wales. Compared against the later Stuarts, Willie was like a fairy child, with rosy flesh and golden hair ; going back at once to the old English type of a royal race. The king, his god-father, had no child, and from his cradle, Willie was marked as heir-presumptive of the crown. Anne was no favourite with her brother-in-law, but her merry and martial son took the warrior's soul by storm. Going one day into Anne's cabinet, the king observed the boy advancing towards him with a little musket. Coming to a halt, the child presented arms.

'What are you doing, my little man?'

'Learning my drill,' the child replied, 'so that I may help you to beat the French.'

Looking at him an instant, William took him on his knee :

'Have you any horses yet?'

'Yes,' he answered; 'I have one live horse, and two dead ones.'

Smiling at the boy, the king returned:

'But soldiers always bury their dead horses out of sight.'

When William went away, the child had a hole dug in the garden, and buried his wooden horses out of sight.

Pleased with his reply about the French, William at once installed him as a Knight of St. George.

As the next living male heir, the little prince is settled at Windsor; with his nurse, his usher, and four Eton boys as playmates. Anne, his mother, takes up her abode in the royal house, to watch his training, and fidget over his boyish tricks. On the boy's arrival, he parades the gallery, the stairs, the guard-room, and St. George's hall. 'Here,' says he, stopping, 'is the place to fight my battles.' Glancing at Verrio's 'Legend of St. George,' the little knight approves of the Black Prince, as one who had really 'beaten the French.' Calling his own troops to combat, he makes St. George's hall the battle-field; the stair and music-gallery outside, the fortress to be attacked.

One of the Eton boys represents the enemy; nurse and usher are assigned their parts, and both, with much discretion, stand on the prince's side. Small pikes and muskets are distributed, and the enemy takes his ground. One of the boys, whose sheath falls off his sword, lunges the little prince in the neck.

'Halt!' cries the usher, stopping the affray. Blood trickles from the wound, but when the usher asks whether the duke is hurt, he answers 'No!' and pushes after the enemy, up the stairs into the citadel, which they take by storm.

The fighting at an end, Willie descends into St. George's Hall, and looks about among the imaginary killed and wounded.

'Have you a surgeon near?' he asks his nurse. The nurse brings in a pair of bellows, and begins to blow. That is her usual way of treating the victims of Willie's prowess. But he stops her this time with a grave look.

'Don't make a jest of it, for Peter Bathurst hath really wounded me.' No great harm is done, and yet the mettle of the boy is proved.

One day he is taken up to St. George's Keep. The little warrior sniffs and shrugs.

'A keep? Why, there is neither bastion nor

parapet.' He asks to roll down the slope, saying that is what he will have to do when he is a man, fighting in ditch and trench. The nurse and usher can hardly hold him back.

But he is not without reward. A little while ago, he had been the happy owner of four small cannon, given to him by his aunt, which he alarmed his mother by continually letting off. One was burst; the king, his godfather, promised to replace it; but the king is on the Continent, fighting against the French, and has forgotten all about his godson's piece. In the armour-room of the keep, Willie discovers a pretty little model of a piece made by Prince Rupert; this he brings into his mother's presence-chamber, and when his mother enters with the prince, her husband, he salutes her with a round. She smiles her joy and her forgiveness; but the urchin fires a second and a third round. Anne looks very grave. Where can the child have got such heaps of powder? This enthusiasm for the military art must be repressed.

Yet she is quick enough to spoil the child in her own way. Mary being dead, the royal jewels have come to her, but instead of heaping these baubles on herself, she puts them on her boy.

Crowned with a periwig, and all but smothered under a robe of azure blue, the boy is brought into his mother's drawing-room. The George he wears is a present from the king.

'You are very fine,' says his majesty, coming in.

Willie bows his thanks.

'All the finer for you,' explains his mother, addressing William.

Willie is urged to say something in reply, but he stands silent, under his great periwig and mantle, and refrains from saying a word.

These happy days soon fly. At nine, he is supposed to need a tutor and a governor. Burnet and Marlborough are appointed to the posts. As bishop of the diocese and chancellor of St. George, Burnet has a residence in Salisbury tower, in which he lodges more than nine months of the year, attending to his duty, and pushing his interests at the court.

'I took to my own province the reading and explaining of the Scriptures to him; the instructing him in the principles of religion and the rules of virtue, and the giving him a view of history, geography, politics, and government.'

Poor Willie! Two years of the bishop's rules

and principles, politics and government, prove too much for him. He dies under the bishop's hand; and England, resolute against the exiled prince, looks for her future king to George of Hanover, descendant of the Queen of Hearts.

Third in that line of Hanoverian kings is George the Third, so popular in his day as Farmer George. He is a family man, with troops of stalwart boys and girls about his knee; a good and kindly parent, with a trace of quaint old German notions of paternal government lingering in his brain. He looks askance at the big house; shrinking under the feudal towers, the Norman keep, the pinnacles of St. George. A low brick house, with very few stairs to climb, and opening on a heap of shrubs and flowers, agrees much better with his simple tastes. The first George and the second George shrank from Windsor; Verrio's floating figures rather shocked them, and the edifice was too vast for them, if not too sombre for a country-house. Little that is feudal now remains; the Norman tower, in which Surrey sang, and Stradling left his name, is occupied by the housekeeper, and the garrison of the fortress is reduced to a sergeant's guard. The Constable finds the keep too big for him, and his majesty finds the royal house too big for him. Rearing a plain brick cottage, which he calls the Queen's Lodge, he takes up his abode outside the royal ward. The slope, the garden, and the terrace, he can understand. Looking up at the keep, he sighs to think how much of his bunting gets blown away ; the structure is so high, and yet he loves to have that bunting in his sight. He likes a farm, low-lying, fat, and rich, to which he can have a friend to dine on a leg of mutton and a dish of turnips. The friend may be a king ; but it is all the same to this homely man. Not that he has no sense of higher things. He has a little of the builder's art, he has a certain love of books, he has a decided love of science, he has a great respect and veneration for the sacred edifice in the lower ward. Though he shrinks from living at Windsor, like the earlier Georges, he has a mind to take his rest there when his day of rest should come. Walking into St. George's chapel, he finds the floors unwashed, the monuments grimed with dust. He orders soap and water to be brought, and has the edifice cleansed. He has not much sense of poetry, but one is glad to see that he casts an eye on the Lincoln Chapel, and repairs the tomb of Fair Geraldine. For many years the kindly man is part of Windsor ; sometimes he is ill and goes away ; on his recovery, he returns. The people greet him, ring their bells, and let off fireworks, which he watches with the eagerness of a schoolboy. London wits poke fun at him ; dress him in country clothes, and show him huddling in and out of shops in Peacod Street and High Street ; but he goes his way, unheeding their attacks.

His favourite walk is Elizabeth's Terrace. We have many pictures of him, as he walks about that terrace.

One of these pictures shall suffice. The visitor is Burney, Madame d'Arblay's father. After service in the chapel, 'where all is cheerfulness, gaiety, and good-humour,' he walks on the terrace, where he finds the king, dressed in a light-grey, farmer-like uniform.

It is a summer evening scene ; the terrace gay and crowded, deer scampering on the slopes, and 'dears about him everywhere.'

The king and queen, arm in arm, come up.

'How do you do, Dr. Burney ?' says the king : 'why, you are grown fat, and young !'

The queen puts in : 'Yes, indeed, I was very glad to hear how well you looked.'

His majesty pauses : 'Why, you used to be as thin as Dr. Lind.'

Lind, who is standing by, is a lath. The princes and princesses nod and smile. At night, Herschel brings the little music-master back to Windsor for a concert. Music is going on when they arrive ; but king and queen have not yet come in. 'At length,' says the music-master, 'he came directly up to *me* and Herschel, and the first question he asked me was, 'How does astronomy go on ?' I, pretending to suppose he knew nothing of my poem, said, 'Dr. Herschel will better inform your majesty than I can.' With homely humour, George replies, 'Aye, aye, but you are going to tell us something with your *pen*,' moving his hand, as though he were writing on a book ; 'what progress have you made ?' 'Sir, it is all finished,' replies the music-master, 'and all but the last of twelve books have been read to my friend, Dr. Herschel.' George looks at Herschel, and then at Burney. 'I wonder how you find time.' 'Sir, I make time.' 'Make time ! How, how ?' 'I take it out of my sleep, sir.' 'How long have you been at it ?' 'Two or three years, at odd and stolen moments, sir.' The king adds in conclusion, kindly : 'Well,

well, whatever you write will be interesting. I don't say it to flatter you ; if I did not think it, I would not say it.'

When the great worry of his life is over, he finds the resting-place of his heart, in the vault to which he has already gathered his favourite daughter and his affectionate wife.

CHAPTER XXXIV.

HOME.

1838–80.

A THIRD scene—and the last—shows the fortress of Edward, the court of Elizabeth, the camp of Cromwell, the head-quarters of William, changed into the picture of an English home.

This Windsor home—stately and yet domestic —is an outcome of the modern mind. Henry of Richmond gave the first hint towards a country-house, by erecting the Tudor tower; Elizabeth carried his idea forward in her gallery and terrace, which made the garden and the slope integral parts of the royal house.

The work then stopped for more than eighty years; kept back by feudal theories, and the armed resistance to those theories. Even when the fight was over, reigns elapsed before the sentiment of domestic life came into vogue again at Windsor.

In and out among the shires, that sentiment was flowering into country-houses of a noble kind; Chatsworth, Blenheim, Belvoir, Welbeck, sprang into existence. Monastic and baronial buildings were transformed. Wilton abbey became Wilton house; Kimbolton castle put on a Greek portico; Battle abbey became a villa; Sherbourne castle was replaced by a country-house. Ditch, drawbridge, portcullis, disappeared. Doors opened into gardens, windows gave on parks. The free and unfenced aspect of old English country life returned, as in the days before Henry built for Edith the first, King's house on the royal mount. Some of the feudal strongholds—York and Lancaster, Norwich and Nottingham, for example— unfitted for domestic use, were gradually abandoned to the jailer and his men. Was Windsor Castle to become, like Lancaster or Nottingham, a common jail? Or was it, like Wilton and Kimbolton, to be glorified and brightened into a domestic shrine?

The sight of that homely king, who built himself a shed outside the Castle gate, brought up these questions. Men watched that kindly sovereign, arm in arm with his good wife, followed by his manly-looking sons and handsome daughters, wind from the door of his brick cottage on the ridge, pass, like a stranger, through the ward of his own house, and drop to the Terrace on which he loved to take his evening walk. After holding his open-air court on that terrace, they saw him troop away, passing the great house of Edward and Elizabeth as though it were not his; and so, through the ward again, he and his family, to his plain brick lodging on the other side. The sight was painful and unseemly. If another man's heap of granite had been trained to blossom like a rose-garden, why should not his?

The sentiment struck root. Plain king and loving wife were both asleep in St. George's chapel, ere the work began. For many years, masons and carpenters toiled by day and night; yet two reigns passed, and a new reign began, before the feudal fortress was transformed into a country-house, in size, in splendour, and in aspect worthy of the foremost family in the world.

One final touch enchants the house into a home.

A woman's touch is needed, and the woman is at hand; with fancies running on dairies, fruit-trees, bee-hives, kitchen-gardens, and the many wants of a great English house, no less than on the strife of parties and the intrigues of foreign courts. The house is built, the home is to be made.

She comes to Windsor in the heyday of her youth ; with her, a blue-eyed Saxon prince ; bright, winsome, tender ; a companion born and trained, as one might say, to be her guard and guide.   He is a man of no less striking quality than appearance ; learned, staid, and searching ; an orator, an artist, a musician ; yet with homely German notions as to waste and want ; the need of seeing that the kitchen-stuff paid the cost of its production, and the yield of cream and butter paid the wages of the dairy-maid.

Victoria and Albert, young queen, young bridegroom, come to Windsor for the holidays, and have their rides and drives, their lounges on the slopes, their little concerts in the music-room, their little picnics in the forest and by the water-side ; and from the ridge of their lofty hill, they listen, as it were, to the roar of the great Babylon down the river, which brings to them the echoes of other Babylons beyond the Channel and beyond the mountains, in every tale and even tone of which they have a part.   These spiritings from the outer world disturb at times their interest in the ducklings in the pond, and the fowls in the Little park ; but not for long. The healthy nature soon regains her mastery. The queen is busy with her fruit-trees, and the prince is bent on proving that his farms will pay. So, in the open air and country, these two take their rest, and brace their nerves for the supreme activities of life.

A son is born to them at Windsor, that ' Bertie ' of the family circle, who, as Albert Edward, is the heir of royalties and imperialities in every quarter of the globe. The young bridegroom, already Knight of the Garter, becomes Constable of the Keep and Ranger of the Great Park. The wall enclosing the Little park drops down before him ; and the young queen, sitting in her boudoir, finds her view extended, as by magic touch, into the forest glades, and out by Runnymede, across the river into distant woods and pastures.

More boys and girls crowd around their knees. These youngsters grow in height and strength. One goes away, the bride of a young Paladin, to become the mother of a line of emperors. Not of this circle only, but of every circle in the kingdom, that blue-eyed Saxon prince becomes a pattern and a guide. Before the fulness of his life comes out, he is at rest :—the home becomes a shrine.

The central figure in this family group is

veiled. The veil is not without a silver lining, but the veil is here ; a habit of the mind as well as of the physical frame.

No great emotion should be seen too near. To read the story of such a loss, we need some help from time and space. When Queen Victoria has become to the descendants of her people, what Queen Elizabeth is to us—when all the trifles of our time are gone, and only the realities left—the story of her love, her happiness, her loss, will be a favourite theme of poets, artists, and story-tellers. Faith that knows no limit, constancy that clings like life, are not of every age. What will the writers of a coming day, who take this theme for tale and idyl, have to tell ?

They will draw the picture of a young and fatherless girl, called, while in her teens, to occupy the greatest throne on earth ; who had to take her place at the head of a great society, with little or no support from her immediate kin. They will paint her grandeur and her loneliness, in a station which allows no sharer and admits no friend. They will show the Saxon prince who came to her and made himself a part of her ; then, line on line, the story of their lives will be unrolled ; years of domestic bliss, broken at length by sudden snap, in the very noontide of their married joy.

Then may come the pathetic sequel of a sorrow which knows no change—which draws away from the haunts of men—which lays down much of the pomp of royal state, and gives up all the vanities of the world—not in old age, when blood is said to be cold, but in the flush of life, when all the tides of emotion are running high—to nurse in solitude a deep and tender sentiment of personal faith. Millions will dwell with fondness on this story of a human heart ; in which the woman rises to a higher throne than that of Queen.

Battle abbey, iv. 324

Beauchamp, bishop of Salisbury, builds Lincoln chapel, iii. 118

Bedell, chaplain of the English embassy in Venice, iv. 67 ; assists Marco Antonio in his desire to enter the English church, 68

Bedingfield, jailer of queen Catharine of Aragon at Kimbolton, iii. 207 ; has charge of Elizabeth in Windsor Castle, ib. ; Elizabeth's remark to him on his qualifications as a jailer, 251

Bedford, lady, one of the court of queen Anne, iv. 24

Bedford, earl of, passes from the Parliamentary party to Charles, iv. 193, 199

Belvoir, iv. 324

Bentinck, William, has apartments in the Tudor tower, iv. 308 ; his interview with Clarendon, ib.

Bishops, mortality amongst, in the reign of Mary, iii. 247 ; imprisonment of, iv. 154

Blage, evidence given by him against Surrey, iii. 137

Blechingdon house, capture of, by Cromwell's troops, iv. 210

Blenheim, iv. 324

Blount, Elizabeth, mother of Henry earl of Richmond, iii. 73, 75 ; her marriage to Clinton, 75, 271 ; is created by Henry VIII. lady Tailbois and countess of Lincoln, ib.

Boleyn, Anne, her marriage to Henry VIII., iii. 81 ; her friendship to Richmond and Surrey, ib. ; her maids of honour, 82 ; favours the suits of Richmond and Surrey, 85 ; obtains a brief from the pope to sanction the marriage of Richmond with lady Mary Howard, 86 ; conspiracy against her, 90 ; is executed, ib.

Bonner, bishop, is present at the funeral of Henry VIII., iii. 186 ; his fall on the accession of Edward VI., 192 ; feelings of Elizabeth on her accession towards him, 248

Borgia, Cesare, is entrapped by Fernando of Aragon, iii. 34, 42

Bosworth field, battle of, iii. 2, 4, 10, 20

Bourchier, constable of Windsor Castle, holds revels in the Norman tower, iii. 12

Bourne, Dick, bears witness against Surrey, iii. 129

Bowes investigates the matter of the riot of Surrey, iii. 135 ; asserts that Wyat had uttered accusations against Elizabeth, 242

Bray, Reginald, architect to Henry VII., iii. 15

Bray, vicar of, is present at the burning of Filmer, Pearson, and Testwood, iii. 159 ; his resolution thereon, 160

Brentford, iv. 181, 182

Brigstoke park, enclosure of, iv. 15, 16, 17 ; effect of, 17

Briquemault, sent by Condé to Elizabeth, iii. 286 ; induces Rybaud to endeavour to free the four hostages of Calais, 288

Brown, school of, iv. 5

Browne and Marina, iii. 122

Browne, his marriage to the Fair Geraldine, iii. 136, 163 ; investigates the charges against Surrey, 136

Browne, major-general, disagrees with the Commonwealth of Cromwell, iv. 271 ; his arrest and imprisonment, 272

Bucer, his bones dug up and burnt at Cambridge, iii. 252

Buckeridge is indicted for killing the king's deer, iv. 96, 97

Buckingham, Edward, duke of, disgraded from the order of St. George, iii. 61, 67 ; mistakes respecting him made by Shakespere, 61-63 ; his excessive pride, 63 ; his connexion with the royal line, 65 ; is charged with high treason, ib. ; his arrest and execution, 66 ; his banner and crest treated with indignity, 68 ; his daughter lady Bess and his grandson Surrey, 68-70

Burbage, the tragedian, iii. 317

Burnet, bishop, appointed tutor to William, the son of queen Anne, iv. 317

Burney, Dr., his interview with George III., iv. 320

Bushel, Brown, a captive in the Norman tower, iv. 231, 232 ; his execution on Tower hill, 233

THE END.

LONDON:

Printed by STRANGEWAYS AND SONS, Tower Street, Upper St. Martin's Lane

9 783337 039073